ED J. THOMPSON

THE BLACK ROBE

Ed J. Thompson

Copyright © **2025 by Ed Thompson. All rights reserved.**

Published by Winged Publications

Editor: Cynthia Hickey

All rights reserved. No part of this publication may
be reproduced, stored in a retrieval system, or
transmitted in any form or by any means—electronic,
mechanical, photocopying, recording, or
otherwise—without the prior written permission of
the publisher. The only exception is brief quotations
in printed reviews. Piracy is illegal. Thank you for
respecting the hard work of this author.

This book is a work of fiction. Names, characters,
places, incidents, and dialogues are either products
of the author's imagination or used fictitiously.
Any resemblance to actual persons, living or dead,
or events is coincidental. Scripture quotations
from The Authorized (King James) Version.

Fiction and Literature: Inspirational
Christian mystery and suspense

ISBN: 978-1-968792-00-8

DEDICATION

This is dedicated to the brave attorneys and support staff who fight the good fight everyday defending poor and indigent persons caught up in the criminal justice system.

Judges in the United States have been wearing black robes since the early 19th century. The plain black robe symbolizes impartiality and stands for justice and fairness. It is solemn and dignified, and it reinforces the notion that- like the constitutional principles they uphold- judges are neutral decision-makers without bias or hidden agenda.

Chapter 1

I slowly put the phone down and plopped myself down on Carla's sofa. I was in shock.

"What's wrong, Sam?" Carla asked. "What happened?"

"Uh… a friend of mine just died."

"Who?" she inquired.

"His name is Ron Smith. He's from Corn Hill. We were best friends in junior high."

"I'm sorry," she expressed. "How did he die?"

"He was stabbed on a bus. He was a bus driver in Newburgh."

"Newburgh? Where's that again?"

"It's near Poughkeepsie, like an hour north of New York City."

"Right…Did they catch the guy who killed him?"

"I don't know," I answered. "That was my grandmother on the phone. She just said that his sister called her and wanted me to know that Smitty had died."

I leaned forward and put both of my elbows on my knees and my hands on the sides of my head. My insides were churning, and I felt sick to my stomach- so much senseless death.

"When was the last time you saw him?" Carla wondered.

"That's the strange thing," I reflected. "I just ran into him here in Utica about a year ago. He was outside the courthouse on the street when I was getting out of my car. We stood there for about an hour and caught up."

"Gee, that is strange."

"He had two brothers who were both shot and killed here not too long ago."

"You're kidding!"

"He was having a hard time with all of that. I remember thinking how sad and tired he looked."

"I can see why," she sympathized.

"And he was active in his church too. He did tell me that."

"Do you know if he was married?"

"Yeah, he was. I think he said that she was from Newburgh. That's how he ended up moving there."

"That poor woman."

"He had like four or five kids too," I uttered in despair.

"Oh my!" Carla exclaimed and got up from her seat at her desk and cozied up next to me. "This is all so tragic. I wish that … I knew something to say."

"There really isn't anything to say," I lamented. "It's getting harder not to feel hopeless in a world that seems so cruel and calculating. It's always two steps forward and then one step backwards for most of us."

"I know," she echoed.

"But thank you – I love you," I said.

"I love you too," she whispered.

I couldn't help but smile as she kissed my cheek. This was still new for us. We were still just coming back together after our nearly two-month breakup. I felt it in my toes every time she told me that she loved me- something that she couldn't say before, even though we had been together for over a year. It was like music to my ears- and medicine to my wounded heart!

"Can I get you something?" she asked, "Some more coffee?"

"No thanks. I gotta head out soon. I have that men's meeting at the church tonight. Remember I told you?"

"You still gonna go to that?" she asked and shook her head in disbelief.

"Yeah, I really don't have a choice. I promised Elder Jake that I would be there."

"Can't you just call him and tell him that something just came up?" she asked. "I'm sure he'd understand."

"I know, but I think it might help me to get my mind off of …what happened."

"Okay, if you say so," she surrendered. "But I think you're kidding yourself."

"Maybe, but I can always leave if being there turns out to be too much."

The truth is that I really liked my new church. I had been attending there for just five months and I was growing in leaps and bounds. *Resurrection and Life Church* was a small, charismatic, nondenominational church in Marcy, New York. After night court one evening, Judge Wilson, the town justice in Marcy, invited me to visit his church some time and I halfheartedly said that I would. I had looked at several churches in the area in the eight months since I gave my life to Christ, but no place felt right for me. I was getting discouraged.

But there was just something different about this little country church. For one thing, the congregation was ethnically diverse. The membership was only about 20 families, with a few people of color-like me- sprinkled about. The senior pastors were Justin and Marlene Henderson. They were both in their early thirties and phenomenal teachers of the Word of God. They were also white.

To be honest, their race was, in fact, a bit of a hurdle for me to overcome at first, even though everyone had really gone out of their way to make me feel welcomed. Judge Wilson introduced me to several people, including the pastors. Everyone seemed impressed that I was an attorney, and a few made jokes about always needing *a good Christian lawyer*.

However, more than anything, I immediately loved the depth of the teaching. I had never heard anything like it before. It was life to me. I also liked their emphasis on teaching true believers how to experience God for themselves, which was exactly what I needed at that point in my life. I was floundering a bit.

But it still took a few months before I found my bearings there. It wasn't at all the kind of church that I had envisioned for me. However, something inside kept telling me to give it time. Besides, I really had nothing to lose, and I knew that I could leave there any time that I wanted.

As I predicted, my grandmother thought I had lost my mind. That's why I didn't tell her right away. I waited until I was officially a member of the church before I brought it up. It somehow felt wrong to keep it from her after that.

"Why would you want to go to white people's church?" she questioned and gave me the side-eyes look in judgement. "That don't make no sense."

"All kinds of people go there," I commented. "Not just white people."

"If the pastor is white, then it's a white church," she declared. "Everybody knows that!"

"I don't think Jesus cares what color the pastor is," I contended. "God is a spirit, not flesh and blood. He is not about *a color.*

She was sitting on the couch in her living room watching a game show. I had just stopped by her house to bring her a couple of things from the drug store that she had requested. I was standing under the door frame. She suddenly took her eyes off the television and stared at me intently. I knew what was coming next.

"Maybe not, but you should be," she snapped. "They probably don't want nothing from you but your money."

"Mama, that's not fair."

"*Fai*r the fai is in italics, but the r is not you say?" she asked in a huff. "Are you kidding?"

"I'm learning all kinds of stuff that I never knew before," I asserted.

"Like what?" she challenged.

"Like who I am in Christ."

She rolled her eyes. "Give me a break."

"No, it's really good."

"Carla go to this church with you?" she wondered.

"No, she hasn't been yet."

"Hmm…now I see," she replied with a chuckle. "Case you're wondering, I'm with her. That ain't nothin but some mess."

"You don't know what you're missing," I taunted.

"What kinda music they sing?"

"What?" I reacted. "What does that have to do with anything?"

"Cause we sing from the soul and them people don't know nothing about that."

"They sing the same songs that you sing at your church," I asserted.

"Doubtful they got a choir good as us."

"They don't have a choir, just a few worship leaders."

"And you like it?" she pressed.

"Yeah, it's good."

"'Cause you been what you call '*brainwashed*,'" she mocked. "Our music is one of the things that God gave to us. Why do you think white people always stole our music like they stole everything else? There were times when the only thing we could do was sing to God with all our hearts from all our pain."

"A song is a song," I contended. "It shouldn't matter who is singing it."

"My mama used to tell us all the time not to sing with white folks," she boldly spoke. "She said it ruined your voice."

"That's ridiculous!" I dismissed. "And racist. You should be ashamed!"

"No, you the one who should be shame," she countered. "You went to school with them folks all those years and now you think just like 'em."

"Mama, you *do* know that there is only one God- not one god for white people and a different one for us?"

"I don't know any such thing," she resisted. "But what I do know is that white people don't know God the way we do cause if they did, they would treat us better."

"From where I'm standing, it doesn't look like we treat ourselves too good either," I submitted. "We got teenaged gangsters out here shooting each other for sport and selling drugs to other people's kids - destroying our own community!"

"You know that's different," Mama argued.

"No, it isn't," I protested. "Sin is sin, Sister Hicks!"

"Now you really talkin crazy, Sam. I thought I raised you better than that."

Fortunately, I knew how to take my grandmother. I wasn't bothered in the least by anything she just said. Her bark was almost always worse than her bite- although admittedly she tended to bark a lot. I knew how it sounded and that oftentimes she was hard to take.

However, Mama still lived partly in the past. Having grown up in Mississippi before the Civil Rights Movement in the United States, she experienced more oppression being Black, dirt poor and a woman than I ever knew. She carried plenty of scars from wounds inflicted a long time ago that never completely healed properly. Without a doubt, her judgement couldn't be trusted on many matters, especially those related to issues of race.

As for me, I just wanted to learn as much about the Jesus who just saved me as I could. Clearly, there was much to be learned and there simply was no way that I was going to go to one of those churches where the pastors preached "feel good messages" every week that got people excited emotionally and placated, but they still went home essentially unchanged and bound.

Indeed, I knew that I, for one, needed real transformation in my life and I refused to settle for less. I wanted more and I was willing to leave my comfort zone to find it- if that's what it took. I was determined to follow my own path regardless of what anyone else thought about it.

———— • ● • ————

Judge Lombardi died suddenly. Apparently, he had a heart attack in his sleep and never woke up. Of the two county court judges in Utica, he was my least favorite. He was mean and selfish. We had a nickname for him in the public defender's office; we called him, *the monster judge.*" But it was still sad, and I knew that many who worked in the courthouse were devastated by the news.

My boss Teresa Sanders, the Public Defender, closed our

office so that everyone could attend the funeral, and we all sat together. The service was at Holy Family Church, a huge Catholic Church located downtown, not far from the courthouse. The church was full. As I sat there, I was once again reminded of just how different I was from everybody else who worked in the courthouse as mine was the only Black face sitting among the sea of mourners.

There were only two eulogies, one from Anthony Lombardi, the eldest son, and the other from Mike Belmonte, the Judges' former law partner and best friend of 35 years. I had never met either one of them before. Mr. Belmonte was clearly quite torn up and struggled to make it through his remarks. His round face was completely flushed, and his eyes never left his notes. Among other things, he described Judge Lombardi as being *"fair to his core and the consummate jurist."*

•●•

My friend Ron and Judge Lombardi were buried the same week in Utica, having died a couple of days apart. As I watched them lower the casket containing my friend's remains into the ground, my own tortured youth ran through my mind like an old movie. It occurred to me that the two men, who lived in proximity for many years, never met and probably had little in common. But death is the great equalizer in that none of us can take anything with us when we go.

Moreover, we all must stand before God one day and give an account of the things that we have done during the short time that we had on this earth. And we can rest assured that God, the *Eternal King,* and *Righteous Judge*, knows intimately the heart of every man, such that, probably for the first time ever, the rulings and final judgment of the high court will be counted as perfectly fair and just.

Chapter 2

Historically, a coronation is the ceremony where a king or queen is crowned and enthroned. We see biblical sovereigns being crowned in the Old Testament. While the United States is a democracy rather than a monarchy, there are some similarities between the installation of a king and the swearing in of some politicians today into a governing office.

The Oneida County Legislature appointed, in short order, Vito Spinoso to replace Judge Lombardi on the County Court bench. I had never heard of him. He was a real estate and commercial lawyer who was a former republican party county chairman. Notwithstanding the fact that he had never tried a criminal case before in his life, the county bar association, as part of the screening process, found him to be *"highly qualified."* as a judicial candidate.

He was sworn in approximately six weeks after Judge Lombardi died. He was 58 years old and average height and weight. He had a full head of dark brown hair with a hint of grey on the sides. He reminded me a lot of my high school industrial arts teacher and I wondered if they were related somehow. He was married with two adult children and several grandchildren, who were all in attendance. They looked like the ideal American family.

He wore the black robe proudly for the first time as he stood prominently, with his wife by his side, before a packed courtroom of witnesses and took the official oath of office. With his right hand placed on top of the Bible, he swore, among other things, that he would support the constitution of the United States, and the constitution of the State of New York and to faithfully and impartially discharge all the duties placed upon him as a judge. From where I was seated, I thought that I saw tears in his eyes. The whole thing lasted about ten minutes. Thereafter, the entire room erupted in applause.

State law required that a copy of the signed oath be filed in the office of court administration before the new judge can discharge any of his or her official duties. He told the audience during his brief remarks that this was one of the *"most humbling"* days of his life. He said that he only wished that his Italian immigrant parents who came to this country with essentially nothing but the clothes on their backs could have witnessed this moment.

There was a welcome reception for Judge Spinoso in the back of the courtroom after the reception. It felt and looked a little strange to me to see people eating and drinking in the courtroom as I had never seen anyone do that before. Typically, food and drinks were not allowed in any of the courtrooms, and the court attendants aggressively confronted anyone who dared to ignore the prohibition that was clearly posted outside the main doors.

I don't recall anything unusual about our first meeting at the reception. He graciously extended his right hand to me and smiled warmly at me the same way he did for all the other guests and well-wishers present in the room. He just said that he was looking forward to working with me and I returned the sentiment. I was only there for a few minutes.

The first time that I appeared before him in court was also uneventful. It was a sentencing on a guilty plea that Judge Lombardi had taken several weeks before he died. It was my understanding that Judge Spinoso was going to get all of Judge Lombardi's cases, which meant that he had a lot of my cases. Although I never wished Judge Lombardi any ill will, I certainly welcomed the change.

It was two weeks later when I got my first hint that something might be off with this judge. It was during a pre-trial in Judge Spinoso's chambers and I was trying to get the assistant district attorney ("ADA") to give my client a little better offer, which was pretty much an everyday occurrence. There were a few other attorneys from our offices in the room.

"Come on Ted, it just two years," I appealed.

"No way, Sam."

"Look, I know that you don't want to try this case anymore than I do. I'm telling you that my client will take three years. That's still pretty good, considering everyone agrees that your victim started the fight."

"He could have died," Ted said in protest.

"But he didn't. The cut was basically superficial. There is a lesson in this for both of them."

"And I suspect that there is a lesson in this for you too, Mr. Hicks," Judge Spinosa interjected. "See, I'm not one to mince words. The offer stays the same. Your client can take the deal or go to trial. It doesn't matter to me which way it goes."

"What lesson exactly?" I questioned.

"It's simple really," the Judge declared. "They might not be my *monkeys*, but it's my circus now."

"What?" I reacted. "It's nobody's *circus*, Judge. These are real people we are talking about."

"I was just using an analogy," the judge defended. "But I think you get my point."

"I think that maybe I do."

I looked around the room. Everyone looked uncomfortable.

"Good," he said quickly with a strange grin on his face. "Then we understand each other."

I couldn't believe what just happened. I felt like I had just been called out by a bully on the playground... only the bully was the teacher! I was caught so completely off guard that I didn't know what to say or do. I was mostly embarrassed and offended... But I was angry too.

I silently fumed about the exchange for the rest of the day. I played the scene repeatedly in my head. It wasn't just what he said, but also the way that he said it. He had a look in his eyes that I had seen many times before- his contempt for me shined through. I had been singled out for a reason. There was no doubt in my mind that he was sending me a message.

But there really wasn't anything that I could do. He was the judge and I had a large caseload with a lot of people who I was assigned to represent in his courtroom. I needed to keep a clear head and not overreact. I also knew that I needed to just swallow my pride and move on.

When I told Carla what happened with the new judge, her reaction really helped me calm down.

"I don't get it," she pretended. "Who exactly are these *monkeys*?"

"What do you mean?"

"Are these the monkeys that ride the tricycles?"

"Probably not," I played along.

"Really? No tricycles, huh?"

"Pretty sure."

"Well, what other animals are in his circus?"

"I don't know."

"Oh, I used to love the elephant wearing the tiny tiara while sitting down for tea. You think he got one of those?"

"I doubt it."

"What about the boxing bears?"

"Nope," I answered and started to snicker.

"Bearded lady? She's a staple, a must have."

"No bearded ladies in the courthouse," I replied. "There's an older lady who works in the probation department who has a few whiskers, but not a full beard."

"You sure?"

"Yeah, I'm sure."

"Then I don't know, Sam," she derided. "His circus sounds pretty lame to me. Don't nobody want to see that junk!"

We both laughed.

Chapter 3

Every woman needs a sister, especially a Black woman. I knew that I wouldn't have trusted most of the guys I knew - and none of the ones I represented- be consistent with your dashes. Either add a space before and after or don't. with someone who I cared about. In 1990, the gulf between the sexes was as wide as it had ever been. Women still lagged behind men in wages earned and in influence. Sisterhood really was a gift from God.

Carla met Kiana Barnes at work. Kiana was dark skinned with a thick frame and wore her hair in shoulder-length braids that she usually kept in a ponytail. She was from Brooklyn, New York and worked in the sales department at their news station. They were both 25 years old and seemed to have a lot in common. They became fast friends and started spending a lot of time together outside of the station. In fact, Kiana spent more time at Carla's apartment than I did.

I was happy that Carla found a friend she could bond with. She had recently started seeing a therapist in Utica and she seemed to be doing good. But I knew that she wasn't exactly the confident, posed woman who was part of her carefully cultivated on air persona. Rather, she was often troubled, and she was still struggling to hold it together at times.

We hadn't talked much about the sexual assault that she experienced as a teen that first sent her spiraling downward. Honestly, I wasn't that interested myself in the details, although I was willing to listen if she wanted to talk about it. The only thing she told me was that she was a high school freshman, and the boy was a senior. He had forced himself on her in his car after their first date.

She told her mother immediately after she got home, who thereafter confronted the boy's wealthy white parents. But the authorities were never called for some reason. Instead, they all agreed that no charges would be filed, and her assailant would be sent away immediately to a fancy New England boarding school.

I was hesitant to ask her any questions about it. She had a hard time telling me as much as she did, so I decided to not make her go there. In the end, I just wanted to do whatever I could to support her. In that moment, it seemed that she just needed me to be a safe place where she could be herself. I could tell that she was relieved that I knew about it.

But I felt that I had little insight into what was really going on inside of her. Carla had built a fortress around her heart, and it was a miracle that she had let me in this far. Obviously, she was still angry- and I suspected that that was just the tip of it. Perhaps I should have pressed more, but I figured that was what the counselling was for.

Our breakup was hard on both of us. Besides bringing to the surface all my many insecurities, it highlighted the things in my life that I desperately needed to change. Key among these was my tendency to suppress my own pain rather than dealing head on with the problems in my life. That's one of the reasons that I was suddenly running hard after the things of God. I was feeling less burdened lately because I was learning to lean into Him for my help.

However, Carla didn't share my faith in God. Although she wasn't exactly an unbeliever, or hostile to religion, she didn't have a relationship with God. Nor was she particularly open to developing one. I just stayed in my own lane about it. I fully recognized that she needed to find her own way to Him.

— • ● • —

Carla was promoted to weekend anchor/reporter. Kiana went out to dinner with us to celebrate. We went to a small Italian restaurant on Genesee Street in North Utica that she really liked. Kiana thought to bring Carla a bouquet of flowers, something that frankly never occurred to me. It was everything I could do to get myself there as I was starting a trial the next day and I was obsessing about it.

I was mostly a spectator as the two women talked shop, entertainment, and anything else that happened to enter their minds. They were a force. But I didn't mind. I loved seeing Carla so full of life and excited about something. I kept squeezing her hand gently as she engaged with her friend, and she smiled lovingly at me.

"Oh Carla, tell Sam the best part about your wardrobe," Kiana encouraged.

"I get to go to New York and get all new clothes," Carla reported and shimmied with glee.

"Like you don't already have enough clothes," I ridiculed. "Whitney Houston would be jealous of you."

Carla crossed her eyes and stuck her tongue out at me.

"Girl don't listen to him," Kiana remarked. "Divas rule the world!"

"And you know that," Carla agreed and smirked.

I rolled my eyes and took a bite of my antipasto salad.

One thing that I noticed was that Carla didn't really have any doubts about her ability to succeed in her new job. About this she never wavered. She saw the promotion as inevitable. We were different in that way. I was a pessimist through and through. I wanted to be more like her in that way.

After dinner, I dropped Kiana off at her apartment near downtown and drove Carla home. I never stayed with her at her apartment if I had to go to work the next day and, on this weeknight, it was out of the question as I had an early morning planned. Although I was tempted to go inside, I kissed her goodnight at the door and hurried back to my car and drove off into the night.

• ● •

"Sexual Holiness," was the title of Pastor Marlene's message on Sunday. It was good, and I listened intently. But it also made me uncomfortable. Although I believed that the Bible teaches that every believer ought to learn to control his or her body in a way that is holy and honorable to the Lord, I couldn't help but wonder if some Christians were taking some of the related scriptural passages too far.

Indeed, Pastor Marlene taught that any kind of sex, in any form, outside of marriage was sin. She specifically called out what she called "heavy petting" and masturbation. She told a story about a boy who she knew who got addicted to masturbation after watching pornography and who eventually went on to become a teenage father. She said that it was important to talk about things like this in church so that Christians know what the Bible teaches about these matters and to avoid many of the "traps and pitfalls" that the devil sets in our lives.

However, she did acknowledge that God created sex and that it wasn't necessarily a sin. Her passionate argument was that sex is only for men and women who are married and committed to each other. In this regard, she acknowledged that human sexual desire is healthy and normal and that it is integral to our obligation to procreate the earth, as God has commanded.

Upon reflection, I don't know if I had ever represented anyone with a true sex addiction in the three years that I have been in the public defender's office. But I had come across more instances of deviant sexual encounters, violence and abuse than I ever thought I would. One thing that I can say for certain is that the sexual urge in people can be very strong, even at a very young age. It's biological - almost like the need to breathe, eat or sleep.

That being the case, perhaps telling physically grown and healthy humans that they need to take cold showers and pray a lot until the right person comes along to marry is unrealistic and/or cruel. In the time of the early church in the 1st century, the average life expectancy was around 33 years, in part due to high infant mortality. Most girls were married while they were still in their teens. Today, both men and women, having much longer life spans, are marrying later in life, well into their 20s and 30s.

Further, statistically, the current divorce rates for Christians in this country are very much on par with the rates for unbelievers. Thus, the righteous goal can't really be to push young believers into premature marriage covenants with the cute boy or girl from history class or youth camp to avoid sinning sexually and thereby face the higher likelihood of future divorce - not to mention the accompanying trauma.

Indeed, Pastor Marlene said that she was 22 years old when

she got married. Even by modern standards, that's young. In our oversexualized American culture today, that's a recipe for moral failure and crippling guilt for young people who are most likely spiritually immature and, at the same time, wrestling against raging hormones.

Generally, one must know God to please God. Faith grows over time as we experience God. Undeniably, most teenagers and young adults lack both the overall maturity and the financial means to get married. And it's very much the case that most boys and men especially must learn to train the dog. There is nothing godly about sleeping around.

Obviously, I was thinking about my relationship with Carla as I sat there and listened to Pastor Marlene's teaching. Although we were involved sexually, this was not just recreational coupling. I loved this woman with every ounce of my being. I would do just about anything for her and hoped to be with her forever. But apparently in the eyes of my new church, we were committing the sin of fornication.

It goes without saying that we both needed healing in our souls to be in any position to marry anyone - and only God knew just how long that was going to take. So, I didn't know if this really was a lesson in the need to sacrifice my sexuality to God, or whether the Holy Spirit was saying something altogether different.

No offense, but I wasn't necessarily buying everything that Pastor Marlene was saying in her sermon at face value. I needed more time to consider and to seek God in this for myself.

— • ● • —

Kiana called me. She had a question related to her co-worker getting scammed by a home improvement contractor. I referred her to the Attorney General's Office.

"I have another question for you, Mr. Hicks, if you don't mind."

"No, I don't mind."

"Where are all of the brothas?"

"Who?"

"You're from Utica," she pressed. "Where are the brothas? Help a sister out."

"Oh, I don't really know," I replied. "I don't get out much these days. When Griffiss Air Force Base in Rome closed in 1995, it basically took all the young eligible Black guys with it. It has never really been the same here since then."

"Don't you have any friends?"

"Sorry, but the only friends I see on a regular basis are in the county jail," I joked. "I'm pretty sure that you don't want one of them."

"No thank you," she rebuffed. "I can roll down the hill by myself."

I laughed. "Ain't that the truth. Sorry, but I don't think that I can be much help to you."

"You know, I told Carla that I want one just like you," she complimented.

"Like me?" I questioned. "Are you kidding?"

She giggled. "You're the catch of the county, Sam. Don't you know?"

"No, you got it all wrong," I refuted- "I *got* the catch of the county. Have you seen her? Poetry in motion this woman – like waves in the ocean!"

"I like your style man," she said. "What do you say I go to church with you sometime?"

"You wanna go to my church?"

"Yeah, I know that Carla doesn't want to go," she noted. "I'm a church girl myself- born and raised in the Baptist church, thank you very much!"

"I didn't know that."

"Yeah, I used to sing in the choir in my old church in Brooklyn."

"You can sing?"

"Yes, I can blow a little," she revealed with a sly smile.

"You know, this isn't a Baptist church," I cautioned. "It's more charismatic with a mixed congregation of people."

"I know. Carla told me."

"So, if you are good with that, you are more than welcomed to come with me one Sunday."

"Great," she replied enthusiastically. "It's a date!"

Chapter 4

Within the judicial system in this country, it's the judges who reign supreme. For the most part, they have complete autonomy in their courtrooms. They decide who comes and who goes, and when. They can even choose to completely ignore the rule of law altogether in a case if they desire, especially if they aren't overly concerned that a higher court might subsequently overturn their decision.

Judge Spinoso was arrogant, and no doubt a bit of a narcissist too. He loved the attention that he got from the clerks and court attendants. He liked to interrupt attorneys in the middle of an argument and throw his weight around, even though he didn't know what he was talking about most of the time. We were all forced to just stand there and take his abuse.

I supposedly missed a court appearance. I was told by the court attendant that the sentencing of a client convicted after trial of sexual assault was scheduled for 1:00 p.m. I was sitting at my desk in our office at 11:15 p.m. when Judge Spinoso' s secretary called to say that the judge wanted to see me in his chambers.

When I got there two minutes later, the secretary told me to have a seat in the hall and that the judge would see me momentarily. But that wasn't true. He made me sit there for over an hour and didn't call me into his chamber's until 12:20 p.m.

When I walked into the room, he was leaning back in his chair with his legs crossed in front of him and both of his feet on his desk facing me. He had the phone to his ear and gestured to me to take a seat in the chair facing him. He never looked directly at me.

He ended his call after a couple of minutes of ignoring his captive audience of one.

"Mr. Hicks, you failed to show up in my court for a scheduled sentencing today," he spoke. "Can you tell me how that happened?"

"I'm sorry Judge," I begged. "I thought the sentencing was on for 1:00 o'clock."

"Everybody else was here, including your client. Everyone that is, except for you."

"I don't know what happened," I said. "I'm sorry"

"I'm not interested in your apology," he rebuffed. "Do you know how much money you cost the county today because of your inability to keep your calendar straight?"

"I have never missed a court appearance before."

"Honestly, I have a hard time believing that" he admonished. "I've heard that… you know that… culturally… certain people… have a hard time being on time. But I'll have you know that I'll have none of that from you."

"I'm not sure I know what you mean," I said. "Are you…"

"Then let me make myself perfectly clear," he interrupted. He was staring hard and the veins on the side of his neck were protruding. "I want you to make sure that you have your ass in the courtroom before I get anywhere near the bench every time that you appear before me! The next time this happens, I am holding you, and the entire public defender's office in contempt of court and you can tell Teresa Sanders that I said that! Let this be a warning to all of you! Now do you understand?"

"I don't really appreciate the way that you are speaking to me," I somehow managed to say.

"Like I care what you *appreciate*," he chided. "Now you can leave my office."

He immediately put his head down as if he was looking for something on the top of his desk.

I seethed as I rose to my feet. He treated me like a child, or like property he owned. The entire time that I was there, I had a bird's eye view of the bottom of his shoes, which I was convinced was premeditated.

As soon as I got back to my desk, I called Frank Bryant, the court clerk.

"Frank, what happened with the Lewis sentencing today?" I asked.

"Oh, it got moved to tomorrow?"

"But what happened today?" I insisted.

"It was first scheduled for 1:00 o'clock today, but then it got moved to 11:00 o'clock at the request of the district attorney's office. Now it's on for tomorrow at 9:30 am. Why are you asking?"

"When did the time change today?" I zeroed in.

"This morning."

"Well, nobody told me that it was moved to a different time," I complained.

"I'm sorry about that, Sam," Frank said. "We called the jail and told them to bring the prisoner earlier. We probably just forgot to call you too. I'm really sorry."

I could hear my heart beating and feel the blood rushing through my veins. The whole thing was a set up. I was tempted to go back to chambers and confront the judge, but I wisely reconsidered. For one thing, he would probably keep me waiting there for another hour before talking to me and then he would only find a way to turn it around on me anyway.

Teresa didn't say anything at first when I duly reported to her what the Judge told me to tell her and what I had found out about what really happened. She just listened nervously. My impression was that this latest episode wasn't going anywhere. In the end, Teresa said that she would talk to the judge, but I wasn't overly optimistic.

I decided after that I would never be alone with Judge Spinoso again. I wanted a witness to the abuse. Also, I thought that having someone else in the room might help me keep it together and not do or say something disrespectful that might compromise my integrity and get me in deeper trouble. This judge was clearly trying to provoke me.

———•●•———

Like Carla, I got a promotion at work too. I was promoted to second assistant public defender, which didn't mean anything in the terms of authority. It really was a product of time in the former position rather than a reward for good work. But it came with a small pay increase and a lot less fanfare than Carla got. While I didn't necessarily want or need the title, I needed the money. Every little bit helped.

The heightened tensions at work were starting to really get to me. I could feel it in my neck and back, and my sleep was often broken up. When Carla and I were in Jamaica a few months back on vacation, I thoroughly enjoyed the time away. I desperately needed another break from trying to fix other people's problems. When I was there, I almost forgot who I was. It seemed like that was about a hundred years ago.

But it was only a short reprieve. My caseload was continuing to grow, and it seemed like each new client was more difficult than the last. I cringed every time the phone rang on my desk, and I could feel myself starting that slow descent again into the dark abyss. For the first time, I found myself wondering how much longer I could do this job.

On top of everything else, something was going on with my grandmother physically. She was only 65 years old. At 125 pounds soaking wet, she was still able to do anything she wanted to do. Although she had some dental problems over the years, she never really went to see the doctor. I don't ever remember her being sick much - nothing more than an occasional cold or flu.

 She was convinced that apple cider vinegar was nature's miracle drug and took a couple of tablespoons religiously every day. She was very proud of how healthy she was and often boasted that she was doing better than just about all the women she knew her age. Meanwhile, she still drank six cups of coffee a day and loved her red meat, especially bacon.

She was having female problems, which she was hesitant to talk to me about for obvious reasons. She never actually did. Her neighbor told me. I took her to see a doctor and they were running tests. I could tell that she was nervous.

I rather liked going to the monthly men's meetings at the church. I had been to several. They were the first Saturday of every month, which worked out good with my schedule because I didn't have any night courts on Saturdays. The meetings were informal. Oftentimes, one person was chosen to give a ten-minute testimony followed by a group discussion led by Elder Jake, or another leader. He asked me last month if I could give my testimony next time. I reluctantly agreed.

My hesitation was partly because I was still new to the group, and I had only heard three other guys speak before. I knew that I stood out in the congregation and people were interested in hearing about me. Even Pastor Justin mentioned it to me and said that he was planning to be there. But I didn't feel that I was ready. Elder Jake told me to just talk about some of the things that happened in my life and my current relationship with the Lord.

The meetings were held in the main sanctuary, which had a seating capacity of 200 people. There were only about 30 guys there when I spoke. I was a little nervous and I kept telling myself that it was only ten minutes.

I started out pretty good until I began talking about my mother and, to my total dismay and horror, I lost my composure midway and cried my way to the end:

Although my mother was never around for us much when I was a kid; I think that she had a major impact on me growing up. She seemed to resent me greatly for reasons that I never knew.

So, I didn't understand. I thought that mothers were supposed to love their kids, right? We're talking about my *mother*! But she gave me nothing, and that left me feeling sad and unwanted- like an orphan… Some of my earliest memories are of her yelling and screaming at me for no reason... She used to hit me too…I was afraid of her…Thank God for my grandmother because if it wasn't for her, I probably wouldn't be here today... One time, when I was about 5 or 6, my mother made the mistake of slapping me really hard in front of my grandmother and my grandmother literally lost her mind. She jumped up and dared her to hit me again. She told my mother that if she ever touched me again that she would "beat her down to the white meat." And my mother knew she meant it…. But it was all so awful…and dark …and dysfunctional. To this day, I carry feelings of anger and resentment deep in my heart and it's hard for me to trust people. I know that I have to forgive her and I'm trying to... But it's hard, you know…The weight of it is heavy. I swear sometimes it feels like it's sitting right here in the middle of my chest. But I've been feeling it less and less with each passing day since I started coming to this church. I know that God is working on me from the inside out… I know that I am a work in progress, meaning God is not through with me yet…

I spoke without notes. I hadn't planned on saying any of that stuff about my mother. Maybe I just needed to vent, I really don't know. It just kind of came out. I can't honestly say that it felt good to stand up there like a whiny little baby and cry my heart out. Crying was new to me. It felt strange and I resented it too. But I was only beginning my journey towards redemption and wholeness. I was a babe in Christ. Crying is one of the things that babies tend to do. I guess it's true that sometimes one can only trust the process.

The best part was at the end when everyone prayed for me. They formed a circle around me, and Pastor Justin and Elder Jake put their hands on my chest. I knew it was coming and yet it still caught me off guard a little. I tried to just stand there and stay in the moment, and not think about anything. It felt like I had somehow managed to plug myself into an untapped power source -much like an electrical outlet- and I was being super-charged. I allowed myself to be completely present.

At the same time, it was like God was telling me that I wasn't alone anymore and that he would pull me through. To my surprise, I had a sense of excited expectation. I had to fight hard again to keep my composure. God was about to change everything for me! I could feel it in my bones.

Chapter 5

Hasan Stevens was my new client. He was an inmate confined at Marcy Correctional Facility, in Marcy, New York. He was serving a 5 to 15-year sentence for his conviction of various drug offenses in Queens County. Apparently, he stabbed another inmate in the chest last month during a fight at Mid-State Correctional Facility, also located in Marcy, New York, just a couple of miles from my church. As a result, he was facing a new felony charge of assault in the first degree.

I had never been to a state prison before, only to the county jail. This was my first time representing someone who was already in prison. There was a clear difference. For one thing, the prisons are generally much bigger. Marcy CF was a medium-security prison, where the less serious offenders were housed with an inmate population of 1,200.

Secondly, it was harder to get into the prison, even for a legal visit. There was more security, which included a more thorough physical search. It reminded me a little of going through security at the airport. Except that the prison guards were more aggressive.

This was my first time meeting Hasan as I was not present in court the day that he was brought in for arraignment. After the fight, he had been transferred from Mid-State CF to Marcy CF.

They had him in the special housing unit ("SHU"), which was essentially isolated confinement in a single cell that was separate from the general population. There were special rules for SHU inmates, including policies for visitation and exercise. Most of the inmates in SHU were there because they had violated some prison rule and were being punished.

I was brought to a visitor's room in SHU, which was the size of a very small office. There was just enough room for a small table and two chairs. The lighting inside was dim, which contributed greatly to the overall depressing atmosphere. It felt like I was in a hole somewhere in the middle of the earth.

I was sitting there for about 15 minutes when Hasan was escorted inside, and the door was closed behind him. He stood there momentarily looking at me expressionless. He wasn't a big guy -maybe 5' 10" and 190 pounds. He was dark-skinned, and his hair was closely cropped. His complexion revealed the remnants of what was probably a tough bout with acne during puberty. He wore the state-issued uniform- green short-sleeved shirt and pants. His biceps were big and well-defined. I gestured for him to sit down.

"Hi," I said. "My name is Sam Hicks."

Neither one of us attempted to shake hands.

"I'm from the public defender's office. I have been assigned to represent you on the new charge."

He nodded his head, but he didn't say anything.

"You are charged with assault in the first degree. Basically, the indictment says that you intentionally caused serious physical injury to another person while you were at Mid-State. It says that you stabbed Tyrone Bryant in the neck with a homemade sharp instrument... Do you remember this incident."

"Yeah, I remember," he finally spoke.

"You have anything to say about what happened?"

"Not really. Dude came at me, and I stopped him."

"Why did he come at you?" I inquired.

"I don't know."

"Was anybody else there?"

"There was a lot of people in the yard."

"That's where this happened…in the yard?"

"Uh huh."

"Do you know the names of any of the other guys who were there at the time?"

"I wrote all that stuff down."

"Wrote it down where?"

"In my folder."

"Where is your folder?"

"It's in my cell. I meant to bring it with me."

"Can you bring it next time?"

"Yeah."

"Did you get hurt or wounded?

"Just a couple of scratches."

"Did you have a beef with this guy about something?"

"No, I barely knew him. I think someone must have put him up to it."

"Someone like who?"

He shrugged his shoulders and sat back in his seat. Our eyes locked together for several seconds. Clearly, his heart was beating at a pace that was much slower than mine. Thus, we were out of sync, which made everything seem forced and labored and I was already looking forward to getting out of there.

"Okay then, I don't really have any more questions right at the moment," I said. "What about you? Do you have any questions for me?"

"How old are you?" he blurted out.

"I'm twenty-eight." I answered before I knew it. Typically, I didn't answer personal questions from my clients.

"That's pretty young to be a lawyer."

"I guess," I replied. "Is my age a problem for you?"

"Na, man," he said. "I didn't mean anything. It's just that I never had a Black lawyer before. I was just curious is all."

"How old are you?" I followed suit.

"I'm thirty-one."

We looked directly at each other, sizing up one another

"How much extra time am I looking at?"

"It's hard to say now," I answered. "Assault in the first degree is a very serious charge. If you go to trial and are convicted, it's going to be a lot."

"…Right," he acknowledged.

I thought he looked bored.

"Any new sentence will run consecutively. Do you know what that means?"

"Yeah, it gets added on the back."

"That's correct," I replied. "Pretty scary stuff, I know."

"I'm not scared."

I didn't believe him. These guys never admitted to being afraid of anything. It was a defense mechanism. But I probably made a mistake of accusing him of that. I knew better. The first meeting with a client was about trying to establish a rapport.

"I know," I recanted. "It's just that time is life, and the state is trying to take more of your life from you. That's all I meant."

In response, he spontaneously recited, *"No one takes my life from me. I give it up of my own free will. I have the right to give it up, and I have the right to take it back."*

I did a double take. "John 10:18 - I'm impressed, you know

scripture."

"Yes, the gospel of John is one of my favorite books in the Bible," he said.

"Mine too," I disclosed.

Now his whole demeanor changed. He gave me a half smile. "So, you're a believer too," he spoke. "How about that?"

"But I think you might be taking that scripture out of context," I asserted.

"How so?"

"The point is that Jesus, as the Son of God, couldn't have his life taken from him. Rather he laid it down willingly for us. That's not true for us. A lot of Christians over the years have had their lives stolen, including the disciples."

"You're right about that," Hasan affirmed. "I just meant that can't anything happen to me that God, in his infinite wisdom, doesn't allow."

"Hmm…What do you like about it?" I wondered.

"About what?"

"John."

Hasan smiled to himself and stated emphatically, "Because it's there… maybe for the first time… we see Jesus as fully man and fully God."

"And why is that important to you?" I questioned.

"Because in a place like this, sometimes you need a brother, and sometimes you need a father."

"Hmm…I can see how that could be true," I commiserated.

"And for most of my life, I never had either one," he added.

"Me either."

Neither one of us spoke while we pondered our shared predicaments.

He broke the silence, "You know, the Apostle Paul wrote

some of the deepest New Testament doctrine, the stuff about Christians being a new creature in God and how we ought to live, while he was in prison."

"Yeah, I know."

Hasan suddenly sat straight up in his chair before leaning in and speaking calmly, "That tells me that my life still has meaning, and I'm not alone and I have not been forgotten… even though I have made my bed in this hell on earth."

I felt my spirit leap within me, but I didn't react outwardly.

He sat back, crossed his arms in front and continued, "The thing is, a lot of our wisdom comes from our pain because sometimes that's the only way that God can get our undivided attention."

"My pastor recently said one Sunday that '*although God doesn't cause our pain, he does use it,*'" I mentioned.

"Sounds like a wise man." Hasan whispered with a strange, satisfied look on his face that frankly looked out of place.

I was caught up momentarily wondering if this guy was truly as he appeared to be…Then I remembered why I was there.

"Umm…About your case, it's still really early in the process," I stammered. "Let's just take it one step at a time. If you have some notes, I'd love to see them."

"Okay, no problem," Hasan spoke.

"I'll be back soon. We can talk more then."

I extended my right hand this time, and he reached out and took it. Our eyes locked again, silently cementing our partnership.

Never had I ever imagined that any client of mine would be able to offer commentary on the gospel of John. I probably could say the same thing about myself. A few months ago, I didn't know any scripture- or anything about God. Now it was my primary source of strength.

Obviously, the things that Hasan was saying about not being alone in this world resonated with me. Here he was locked in this dungeon called solitary confinement and yet he seemed to have somehow found his peace, something that I desperately longed for. It resonated in my soul. If true, I was intrigued.

Accordingly, Hasan had captured my attention like no other client had before. I felt a connection to him, but I instinctively fought against it. I knew as well as anyone that most of these guys in jail and prison couldn't be trusted as far as you could throw them. Notwithstanding, I couldn't wait to get his prison file so that I could learn more about this believer in Jesus who just nearly killed a man.

Chapter 6

"Can you do me a favor," Carla asked.

"Sure, what is it?"

"Can you hurry up and take Kiana to church with you? The girl is harassing me about it."

"She's not really interested in going to church," I pointed out. "She's just on the hunt for a husband."

"How did you know that?"

"Cause she told me. She asked me if I knew any good men."

Carla laughed into the phone. "I didn't know she did that. But you can't blame a sista for trying."

"I guess not," I conceded. "You should come with us."

"I don't think I'm ready for all that."

"I know you said that before, but can you tell me why?"

"I just feel like it would be too much for me now. Too much… pressure… I don't know how to explain it."

"Okay. You know that I'm not trying to pressure you into doing anything that you don't want to do."

"I know that Sam."

"I just really think it would help you to heal inside," I suggested. "That's what it's doing for me."

"But we're not the same," she pointed out.

"Yeah, I get that."

"Kiana has been going to church her whole life. She used to sing in the choir."

"She told me that too."

"So, can you call her, please?"

"Okay, not a problem," I relented.

"Thank you."

"But I already told her that I'm like the only Black single guy there."

"Maybe she's also looking to '*heal inside.*'"

"Maybe, as long as she knows that the only eligible bachelors in Marcy, New York are doing time *inside* the big house."

———•●•———

I arrived at Kiana's apartment at 10:30 am. Usually, we just dropped her off and I never got out of the car. I walked up to the door and knocked twice. She was ready, unlike Carla who loved to keep me waiting. But Kiana didn't wear as much makeup and jewelry as Carla did, so I suspected that she didn't need as much time to get dressed. She wore a white ruffled blouse, a plain black skirt and flat shoes. She said that she just needed to get her coat and her Bible.

We sat near the front, as was my custom. I could hear her singing next to me during worship and she really did have a nice voice. I instinctively kept my voice down because I didn't want her to hear me singing off key. Pastor Marlene taught that morning and it seemed to me that Kiana was enjoying the message.

After service, I introduced Kiana to several people, including Pastor Marlene. They spoke for a few minutes, and I walked away for some of it because I didn't want to intrude. I really did want

Kiana to like my church. Hopefully, she would say good things to Carla.

I always stopped after service at Manny's, a small diner located about two miles from the church. Sometimes I ordered takeout, but I liked to eat there better. They had great burgers. A lot of church people went there. I invited Kiana to brunch, and she readily accepted my invitation.

As I drove past the correctional facility, I thought about my conversation with Hasan, and I was saddened a little. I couldn't imagine what it was like for him. Just the monotony of repeating the same thing every day with nothing new to look forward to doing seemed unbearable. Clearly, people are highly adaptable, and we have been made to endure pain- no doubt something worth keeping in mind.

The diner was crowded when we got there, and we had to wait about fifteen minutes before we were seated.

"What do you recommend, luv?" Kiana asked.

"Everything is pretty good. I hope you aren't on a diet."

"No, I'm not on a diet, even though I probably should be on one," she reflected. "But I could go for a nice julienne salad."

We were both quiet while we read the menu. I ordered a bacon cheeseburger with the works and French fries with brown gravy. She ordered the soup and salad special.

"So, what did you think of the service?" I eventually asked.

"Oh, I thought it was good. The people were really nice."

"Yes, they are," I agreed. "As you saw, we are not very big. Makes it easy to get to know everyone."

"So, no choir?" she observed.

"No, there's just a worship team."

"Does anyone ever sing a solo?"

"Not that I've seen."

"Oh, that's probably good," she remarked. "Everyone knows that most of the hell in the church mostly begins in the choir."

"I hadn't heard that."

"It's true," she contended and rolled her neck about. "Creative people have a hard time getting along with each other-especially creative Black folk!"

"What did you think of the message?"

"She's pretty good," Kiana said. "There wasn't a whole lot of women speaking from the pulpit on Sundays in the Baptist churches where I come from. That's the Black church for you."

"But I think that's changing," I offered.

"I don't know."

We ate in silence for a minute. "Did Carla tell you that she's thinking about applying for this job in the city?"

"In New York?"

"Yeah, it's big time. Like with an ABC affiliate."

"No. This is the first that I'm hearing about this. She just got a promotion."

"But this is next level."

"We just got back together and now she's thinking about moving halfway across

the state?"

"I said she's just thinking about it," Kiana defended. "Doesn't mean anything. She could apply for it and still not get the job. I know that it's important in her field to get her name out there."

"Still, it makes me feel like…"

"Look, I probably shouldn't have said anything about it," she interrupted. "It's

none of my business. Just please don't tell her that I told you about it. I'm sure that she's just waiting for the right time to bring it up."

Unfortunately, I was bothered by the fact that Carla was already considering relocating to New York City. Honestly, I wasn't sure if I had a right to be upset or not. It just seemed that in many ways Carla and I were just where we started- with her calling all the shots and me left reacting.

At least, I now trusted that I mattered to her. We had something undeniably special. We both knew it. But I just could never fully relax about us out of fear that everything could change in a blink of an eye. It made me feel weak and passive. But that really was my issue and not something that she was responsible for causing or fixing.

I decided that Kiana was right, and Carla was probably just putting out feelers and considering her options. After all, she was young and talented and needed to follow her dreams. That being the case, I needed to not worry about it and just wait for her to talk to me about it if it became something. Ultimately, a long-distance relationship for us wasn't insurmountable- just bothersome. We could make it work if we had to.

• ● •

Carla's sister had a miscarriage. Christina wasn't quite at the first trimester yet and she hadn't told anyone in the family about the pregnancy, except for Carla, who promptly told me. Carla was really upset and called me at work.

"I know that these things happen all of the time, but I just feel so bad," she cried.

"How is Christina?"

"She's okay. We both had a good cry."

"Maybe, you can go to Rochester and see her," I suggested.

"I thought about that, but I can't go until after the end of the weekend."

"It's already Thursday. That's just a couple of days."

"Yeah, I know…It just seems so unfair, you know. Christina would have been a wonderful mother."

"Yeah, I'm sure that she would have."

"And my parents would have lost their minds with a grandchild to spoil. Can you imagine? I had it all planned out in my head and now it's gone."

"Not forever, just for now," I tried to sound encouraging. "They are both young."

"Let me ask you something," she presented. "Do you think that God lets things like this happen as punishment?"

"Punishment for what?"

"I don't know… Anything and everything."

"No, I don't think that's true," I answered. "Bad things happen every day to good people because we live in a fallen world and God isn't the reason that the world is the way that it is. It's not his fault. We must learn to get through…together. That's his plan."

"How can you be so sure?"

"I'm learning that there are only a few things in life that we can be certain about and one of them is that God is love. He doesn't just love us, he *is* love- his very nature."

She didn't respond immediately. But I could feel her thinking. So, I didn't intrude.

"I just wish it was different, that's all," she slowly whispered.

"Me too."

More silence.

"Thanks, Sam. I needed to talk to you."

"I'll always be here for you, you know," I boldly stated.

"Will you really?" She sounded slightly skeptical.

"Yes, I will… I promise... I told you before that you have changed everything for me. Do with that what you will."

Chapter 7

Whenever anyone from our office had something big going on with one of our cases, we all tried to support each other as best we could. It's hard doing this job alone. Larry had been talking about his child endangerment case for months. I knew that he had worked hard on getting this deal. I made sure to be there for its conclusion.

Shawntay Pitts, age 21, was charged with reckless endangerment in the first degree, stemming from an incident where her three-year-old son was found walking in the middle of a busy street in Cornhill wearing only a t-shirt and a diaper. The temperature was 45 degrees F. Fortunately; the toddler was unharmed. A passerby rescued the boy and drove him to the emergency room at St Luke's hospital.

Shawntay was found high on crack cocaine, intoxicated, and passed out on her sofa enabling the child's escape. There was a lot of press coverage centering around the alleged failure of the Department of Social Services to intervene earlier on the boy's behalf, considering numerous reports of neglect. After months of back and forth, Shawntay pleaded guilty to one count of endangering the welfare of a child, a misdemeanor.

She was scheduled to be sentenced to 6 months in jail before Judge Spinoso, which meant that she wouldn't have to spend any more time in jail. Even looking at her through the most critical of lenses, Shantay looked pitiful. She wore an orange jail jumpsuit, and her short hair was messed about her head. She was shaking nervously, and she hunched her shoulders and lowered her head in a feeble attempt to disappear from creation like she never existed at all. It also appeared that she was sobbing softly to herself, although it was hard for me to get a good look at her face from where I sat on the opposite side of the courtroom, which was mostly empty except for a few press people.

"Counsel, is there anything else before I pronounce sentence?" Judge Spinoso inquired midway through the proceeding. He sat perfectly upright like a king perched on his throne as he cast his eyes downward.

"No, your honor," Joe Bartolotta, the assistant district attorney ("ADA"), said.

"No, your honor." Larry followed.

Without ever really looking directly at Shantay, the judge adjusted his glasses and began reading from his notes:

"The first thing that I want to say to you young lady is how lucky you are. You are lucky that a good Samaritan found your son and he didn't get hit by a car and die by the side of the road that day. You are lucky that the district attorney's office agreed to reduce the charge from a felony to a misdemeanor, so you won't have a felony conviction on your record. And you are lucky that this court agreed to accept that reduction because I didn't have to go along with any of this. As far as this court is concerned, you are a disgrace as a mother. I have read the pre-sentence report, which I accept, in its entirety, and it would appear you have been given ample opportunity to get yourself on the straight and narrow and time and time again you have shown your desire to keep putting your own selfish needs above those of your son. I am sorry to say that this court is not moved in the least by the fact that you were in foster care as a child yourself. That just tells me that you should know better because you know firsthand what it feels like to be abandoned. So now the state must take over the care of your son too. This is your last chance as far as I'm concerned so I hope that you have learned your lesson and use this opportunity to turn your life around somehow and do right by your son. There will be no more coddling. If you are ever before me again with anymore of this foolishness, you should bring your toothbrush with you because I will do everything in my power to keep you from seeing the light of day for as long as possible ..."

Perhaps Shawntay deserved society's wrath and then some, it's hard to say. The judge was right that her gross negligence could have had deadly results. But there is a clear distinction between tough love and all out vengeance. This was hard to watch and by the end of it, I had taken my eyes off the judge, and I was bent over in my seat looking at the floor. It somehow felt wrong being there and I just wanted it to be over.

Judge Spinoso was pridefully cold-hearted, and his words were mean and spiteful. He had a satisfied look on his face as he got up, glanced in the direction of the news reporters and left the bench. It occurred to me that he was ten times worse than Judge Lombardi had been. I guess it's true what they say about being careful about wishes.

Larry and I walked out of the courtroom together. Neither one of us spoke as there really was no need for words. We both already knew. So, we just carried the weight of it together.

Donnie Freeman was one of those guys who thought he knew everything. Talking to him was like talking to the wall. In fact, I preferred the wall because at least it didn't talk back. Suffice it to say, ours was not a relationship made in heaven.

Donnie was 28 years old. He looked older, no doubt a casualty of years of running wild on the Utica streets. He had been in and out of jail since the age of 16, although he only had one felony conviction on his record that resulted in him serving a little over a year in state prison.

He was charged with attempted murder. Apparently, he got into an altercation with another man in a bar. Thereafter, he went to his car, got a gun, and shot the man. Fortunately, the bullet hit the upper right arm, and the injury wasn't life threatening.

I wanted him to take the plea deal offer of 2 to 4 years. He flat out refused. We argued about it for months.

"They ain't got nothin on me!" Donnie vehemently maintained and shot me the deadliest of looks.

"What are you talking about?" I questioned. "A whole bar full of people saw you shoot him."

"Don't matter. That fool deserved what he got."

"But do you understand that if you are found guilty that you are facing 5 to 15 years in prison at minimum."

"I already told you man. I ain't pleading to nothin," Donnie maintained. "How many times I got to say it?"

I eventually got the message and started preparing to try this awful case- in front of Judge Spinoso, no less. Our defense was that Donnie was acting in self-defense. I knew it was weak and a long shot, but at least it passed the laugh test. Most of the time, we didn't even have that.

I went to the county jail three times during the week leading up to the trial to see Donnie. We went over his testimony several times. He seemed to get it. Key was that he had to testify that he reasonably feared for his life. Without it, our defense crumbled like a house of cards.

I thought that the start of the trial went as good for us as I could have hoped. We even had a Black person on the jury, which was a first for me.

I hadn't anticipated how poorly Robert Jones, the victim, would testify. He was a short, stocky guy in his 30s with bad teeth. He also had a speech impediment that made it hard to understand what he was saying. Moreover, he could barely remember what happened before he was shot. He wasn't exactly a sympathetic figure.

Only the bartender positively identified Donnie by name as the shooter, but even he didn't know why or any of the facts leading up to the fight. He testified that he heard them arguing and the single gunshot. He never saw the gun, but he did see Donnie run out of the bar.

I called Donnie as my first and only witness. After asking him about the early part of the evening, I zeroed in the critical part of his testimony:

Q. What happened after you and Mr. Jones were separated?

A. I walked away and went to the other side of the room. I didn't want to beef no more. I could see that the dude was looking to mess with me.

Q. So, what happened next?

A. I left.

Q. Where did you go?

A. I walked to my car. But I couldn't find my keys. I figured they must have fell out my pocket while we was pushing each other and what not and I decided that I had to go back inside the bar to look for them.

Q. And did you go back inside?

A. Yeah. I kept something in the car, under the seat just in case I got into a little trouble you know, and something went down. I got it and…

Q. By *something*, you meant a gun? You got your gun?

A. Yeah. It was underneath the seat, and I got it just in case this dude, you know, tried to start some s**t with me again.

Q. Can you tell this jury what happened next?

A. Yeah. As soon as he saw me come in, he came runnin over to me and started beefing or whatever.

Q. And?

A. And I didn't know what to do, you know what I'm say'n? I tried to tell him that I was just looking for my keys and that's when I slipped and fell?

Q. You slipped? How?

A. I don't know for sure. I think that maybe the floor was wet or something, and as I landed on the floor the gun just fired.

Q. What do you mean it just fired?

A. It went off by itself.

Q. And you didn't pull the trigger?

A. No.

Q. How did it do that?

A. I don't know.

Q. So, you never intended to shoot Mr. Jones?

A. No, I didn't. Like I said, I wasn't looking for no trouble. It was an accident.

This was the first time that I heard this account of how the shooting took place. He was supposed to say that Jones rushed him from behind and that he feared for his life. But what he described was not self-defense. I wasn't sure what it was. I didn't know what to do.

John Fisher, the ADA, had his way with Donnie on cross examination. It was pathetic. Donnie sounded ridiculous trying to explain how a handgun in his pocket discharged on its own. The jig was up. I was mortified.

Judge Spinoso called for a ten-minute recess just as Donnie got off the witness stand. He said that he wanted to see John and me in chambers. He was seated behind his desk when we walked into his office together. As soon as he saw me, he erupted in laughter. His face reddened from the force of it, and he started coughing uncontrollably as he struggled to say something to me.

"Oh, what a tangled web we weave," he finally sang out. He was waving his finger at me.

The reason for this show of spontaneous, uncontrollable glee was completely lost on me. He had inherited this case from Judge Lombardi, and he wasn't involved in any of the pre-trial proceedings. I looked at John and he looked back quizzically. The looks of confusion on our faces caused the judge to suddenly come to himself.

"I almost thought you had us," he said with a straight face. "I really did."

"Who is *us*," I inquired.

"What?"

"You said *us*. To whom is the court referring*?*"

"You know what I mean," he defended. "Are you accusing me of something?"

"No, not at all. I was just asking for clarification."

"Maybe you care to *clarify* why you just tried to offer false testimony in my courtroom," the judge demanded.

"I did no such thing," I insisted.

"What would you call it then?"

"I'm sorry, but I really have to speak with my client," I spoke.

I turned abruptly and walked out of the room. I had grown tired of this abuse, and I knew that I needed to leave before I said something that I would later regret. This was serious business to me, and I had to keep my focus. Afterall, I still had a trial to go out there and lose in the most embarrassing of ways.

The remainder of the trial was a bit of a blur. It took the jury less than an hour to convict Donnie of attempted murder in the second degree. Subsequently, Judge Spinoso sentenced him to 6 to 12 years in state prison.

Chapter 8

Hasan walked through the door carrying a big manila folder that appeared to be stuffed with papers two or three inches thick. He waited until I nodded for him to have a seat before sitting down. It had been almost a month since our first visit. I had forgotten how dark a place it was.

"Let me first apologize for how long it's been since we last met. I had a trial that took up most of my time."

"No need to apologize," Hasan replied. "I know you have other cases, Mr. Hicks."

"Please call me Sam."

"No, I rather not," he answered abruptly.

"Huh?"

"The Bible says to give honor to whom honor is due."

Once again, I was caught completely off guard by this man. He almost seemed out of place.

"I don't mind really," I replied.

"But it's not right. I want to be sure to give you your respect… If that's okay?"

I looked hard at him for a few seconds before lowering my eyes. He had a different kind of vibe going on than I was used to.

"If it's that important to you."

"Thank you," he said.

"So, how are you doing?' I quickly pivoted.

"I'm good."

I gestured toward the folder, which he had placed on top of the table.

"What's all this?"

"My work," he answered. "It's how I spend a lot of my time."

"You writing a book or something?"

"No, but I like to research things."

"I know you did good in school. You taught yourself how to read at what- three years old?"

"No, my father taught me."

"I thought your father wasn't around much," I recalled.

"He wasn't. He was what you call 'a rolling stone.' What else did you read about me?"

"I know you have a very high IQ."

"Lot of good it did me," he dismissed. "Who wants to be the smartest guy in prison?"

"It's still a gift," I asserted and shrugged. "It's how you use it."

"Really?" he resisted. "Cause I used it to sell drugs."

"More like you didn't use it, instead you chose to sell drugs," I refuted.

"It's a part of the game people play and the way of the world," he explained. "I had no choice. We needed the money. We had to eat- me, my sister, and my mother. There wasn't any other way."

"I see."

"Do you?" he questioned. "Almost everyone who I did business with were full grown adults. Most were a lot older than me. They came to me. I never had to go looking for anyone."

"Hey, I'm not judging you," I defended. "Remember, I'm on your side."

"Well, I judge myself," he contended. "And the way I see it, I just played the hand that I was dealt. It just wasn't a very good one, so I lost."

"So, you're proud of all you did?" I pressed.

"Hell no!" he expressed. "All I'm saying is I was bound to lose eventually. All the odds were against me."

"I see."

It's mostly a young man's game out there," he reflected. "You are only young once. Eventually, we all time out one way or another. That's the part that I couldn't see."

"I have to say that you don't really sound too angry about it," I commented. "You seem to have come to peace about everything. If it was me, I would be out of my mind."

"Oh, but I am," he corrected. "I'm angry as hell."

"Then I don't get it," I stated flatly. "Is this you doing that thing where we talk ourselves into accepting the things that we can't change? Because I don't think that really works for most people, especially Black people. Just makes us bitter, and even more of a social outcast."

He slowly shook his head back and forth before saying, "The Bible tells me that

it's okay to be angry, just watch what you do with it."

"Yeah, I know, but..."

"It's really as simple as that for me," he continued. "I try every day to release a little more of it back into the atmosphere where it came from."

"Does it work?" I asked.

"Sometimes, but not always." He was looking at me, but I could tell that in his head he was someplace else.

"So, what are your regrets? If you don't mind me asking."

"Hmm...I wish I was born in Upper East Side with the

Rockefellers and the Kennedys," Hasan joked.

"Don't we all?"

"It's just that most wishes don't come true when you are poor and Black," he waffled.

"I'd say that is true for all poor people because poverty is a curse," I asserted.

"I don't disagree."

"Sometimes it seems that God is missing in action," I lamented.

"God is not our genie, or I wouldn't be here at all."

"But he is all-powerful," I argued. "He can do whatever he wants."

"And we are all disobedient children," he replied. "I put myself here, not God."

"So, you're not mad at God?" I wondered. "Not even a little?"

"Nope."

"I see."

"I've just had it with prison life."

"Speaking of which, tell me about this guy you are charged with stabbing," I redirected.

He sighed heavily and looked away. "It was a planned hit on me. I told you."

"Why do you say that?" I pressed.

"We were all in the yard, but I was the only one attacked by someone who I didn't even know."

"The yard is where you all go to work out?"

"I go every day at the same thme to, you know, work out and to let off some steam," he disclosed. "There was a lot of people there, including some guards. That day I knew something was off, although I couldn't quite figure out what it was. I could just sense it, you know."

"Really?"

"Yeah, I believe that the Holy Spirit will warn us about trouble to come if we are sensitive to it."

"How so?" I questioned.

"I was sitting on the weight bench just resting between reps. That when this here young gun came at me with a shank. We didn't have any words, I mean nothing. He jumped me and I fought him off."

"You didn't know him at all?" I questioned.

"No, that's what I'm trying to tell you," he argued. "I've seen him, but he's not anyone that I would associate with. Somebody put him up to it. I know it."

"No one made any threats against you?"

"No."

"Interesting."

He raised both eyebrows. "The thing about life here behind these walls is that you always have to watch your back because nothing makes sense in here. A guy can go completely off the deep end at the drop of a hat."

"Hmm."

"There is almost like a dark spirit over everybody- including the people who work here," Hasan articulated. "You can never really know what anyone is thinking. It's a crapshoot, if you know what I mean."

"I think I get it," I replied.

"I just thank God for protecting me."

"Definitely seems like He was watching over you," I admitted. "Hate to think what could have happened."

"I felt protected," Hasan articulated. "It was completely unprovoked on my part… It may have had nothing to do with me at all."

"What do you mean?"

"I don't know who got beef with me about something stupid. I try to mind my own business. I have never gotten a ticket in here for anything."

"Yes, I saw that in your disciplinary record."

"All I ever do is go to my program and play chess. That's it."

"You really haven't heard anyone say?" I pushed. "Nobody told you anything?"

"Right after the fight I was taken out of gen pop. I haven't been able to talk to anyone about what happened."

"Did you bring the list I asked you for?"

"Yeah, here it is," he said and pulled a piece of paper out of his folder and handed it to me. "But it's not gonna make any difference. Nobody is gonna talk to you."

"What about the guards? You said that some of them were there."

"Doubtful," Hasan ventured. "They're basically pretty useless."

"What do you think I should do then?" I asked.

"I don't know. Get the tape."

"Video?"

"There's got to be one," he maintained. "Otherwise, it's really just my word against his."

"That's true," I agreed. "But he's the one who almost died."

"But I could have died too if it wasn't for the Lord. He's on my side in this."

Chapter 9

Kiana wanted to go to church with me every Sunday. According to Carla, Kiana didn't have a reliable car and needed a ride. I wasn't thrilled exactly but I didn't really mind, although I didn't necessarily want to go to brunch with her every week.

I almost died the first time that someone asked me if Kiana was my girlfriend. I wanted to immediately march up to the platform and make a formal announcement in front of the entire congregation that Kiana and I were not dating. I know how that sounds, but I wasn't having any of that.

Kiana said that she was thinking about joining the worship team, which I encouraged her to do. The only problem was that she needed to be able to get to the midweek rehearsals. Obviously, I was in no position to transport her to those. She needed to work it out herself.

I also was a little concerned that she was starting to get a little too familiar with me. She would occasionally call me "luv" or "honey." While the nice lady at the dry cleaners did the same thing, it sounded very different to me when Kiana did it. It was more like the sound of fingernails on a chalk board.

———•●•———

Carla did end up going to Rochester and spending a couple of days with her sister after the miscarriage. She only called me once while she was there and came back in a pretty good mood. She said that Christina only needed a day or two to grieve her loss. Being a nurse apparently helped her to process everything quickly.

"I'm glad that Christina is doing good, but how are you?" I solicited.

We were having dinner at Pavones's, home of our favorite pizza in Utica.

"I'm good," she stated. "I was just really worried about her, you know."

"Yes, but you were talking too about your own plans for this baby."

"I know," she conceded. "I know that I got a little ahead of myself there. We really didn't talk about it a lot. Christina is so strong. I wish I was more like her."

"I think that you are stronger than you think you are."

"You keep saying that."

"It's true."

"I don't know, but I like hearing you tell me that," she stated. "I don't want you to see me as this eggshell of a person who can't deal with the everyday pressures of life."

"Nobody sees you that way." I maintained.

"My mom and dad do. Especially my mom. She just looks at me sometimes with such concern in her eyes. It bothers me that I have caused her pain. She doesn't deserve that."

"Your mother loves you," I responded. "You should take comfort in that. My mother doesn't even know my name. She used to call me '*you boy*' sometimes because she couldn't remember who I was."

She laughed out loud.

"Go ahead. You laugh."

"My poor Sam."

"So, see, it could be a lot worse," I asserted. "Your family is there for you. It's a blessing, not a curse."

"You say this stuff about your mother like it doesn't really bother you, but I think it's unprocessed trauma."

"Maybe."

"I want to meet her," she declared.

"Who? My mother?"

"Yeah, I want to meet her."

"I don't think that's a very good idea," I reacted. "Remember what happened when you first met my grandmother? One of the most embarrassing moments in my life, I kid you not."

"Yeah, but we're buddies now."

"That's because you bribed her with all that stuff you bought for her in Jamaica. Now she likes you better than me. You can't possibly feel good about that."

"It worked, didn't it?"

"Yes, it worked," I admitted. "But Janet Hicks is next level."

"So, you think she won't like me?"

"She doesn't even like herself," I explained. "I already told you that my mother is buck-wild. Knowing her, she'll probably show up wearing a see-through animal print bikini and a tiara, like she's 'Laquita queen of the ghetto.'"

Carla chuckled. "That would be unprocessed trauma too."

"Yeah, for me!" I declared.

"Okay, but you can't hide her forever."

"Watch me!"

"Stop Sam, I'm being serious." she reprimanded.

"You can't blame a man for trying to protect the girl he loves."

"Uh, I don't know about that."

"You gotta trust me on this," I begged. "You might not want to pick up the pretty black cat, she doesn't seem to like it very much."

"Alright, if you say so."

"I do."

"Hey, I got a great idea!" she suddenly exclaimed.

"I can't wait for this."

"How about we stay up all night watching these movies I rented?" she solicited. "We can cuddle together and fall asleep together. And tomorrow I'll make you the best breakfast you have ever had in your whole entire life."

I smiled big.

"Is that a yes?" she teased.

"I'm all the way in, most definitely," I expressed. "Just don't shoot me if I fall asleep before the night is through."

"But don't you always?"

I stuck my tongue out at her.

It was a great night. I loved being with her. It felt like we were the only two people on the face of the earth- like when we were on vacation together in Jamaica. I could hear her heart beating as we pressed together. And I could feel myself falling in love with her all over again.

Suffice it to say, however, we didn't like the same kind of movies. She liked foreign films with subtitles and spy plots full of international intrigue. They were really over my head. I hung in there as long as I could, but I eventually drifted off to sleep.

True to her word, she made an awesome breakfast the next

morning. I loved pancakes and she had somehow learned to make them the way that I like- not too thick and a little crispy around the edges. It was Saturday so I didn't have to rush out. She didn't have to go to the station until later.

"Do you want some more coffee?"

"Thanks, just top me off," I replied as I sat at the kitchen table in my t-shirt and boxers stuffing my face. "Everything is delicious."

"Good. I'm glad you like it."

"You should open up your own diner," I not-so-innocently spoke.

"Funny, Kiana said the same thing," she replied matter-of-factly. "Except she thinks I should open one up in Brooklyn."

"Brooklyn?"

"Yeah, she got all excited telling me about it," Carla related. "At first, I thought she was just kidding, But I guess her favorite breakfast place is there, and she knows the perfect spot for a new one."

"You think she was serious?"

"I don't know what she's thinking sometimes," she stated. "Even if I was interested, and I most certainly am not, I don't have any money to open a restaurant. She even found this announcement for a job at a station in New York that she thinks would be *'perfect'* for me."

She looked baffled.

"*She* found it?" I questioned.

"Yeah, she was just daydreaming," Carla offered. "She tends to do that."

"Maybe she's looking to get you out of town for some reason," I suggested.

"Maybe. The thing is she's a better cook than me. Sometimes

I wish that she focused more on her own life."

———————• ● •———————

Kiana called me. She had a question about something that Pastor Justin had said during his message on Sunday. I started to confront her about the stuff she said about Carla moving to New York, but I decided to just let it go. I didn't see what I had to gain by getting into it with her at this point- no harm, no foul.

She did finally join the worship team. One of the other singers agreed to transport her to and from their rehearsals. She was a natural and seemed to enjoy it, especially the added attention from the congregation. She and Tyrone, the young kid on the drums, were the only Black people on the team. My hope was that she would become less dependent upon me as she got to know more people. I saw this all as a good sign.

Chapter 10

The doctor said that my grandmother needed to have a hysterectomy. Apparently, she had three uterine fibroids the size of golf balls, which were the source of her sudden pain and bleeding. There was no way of knowing how long they had been there. According to the nurse at doctor's office, for reasons unknown, Black women have higher rates of hysterectomy and complications compared to white women, Asians, and Latinas.

The good thing is that she didn't have cancer. I gather many post-menopausal women have fibroids Although it was considered a major surgery, women don't die just from having hysterectomies. We were told that she could expect a full recovery in six to eight weeks following the surgery.

However, the diagnosis sent her almost immediately into a depression. I could see the fear in her eyes, and she withdrew completely into herself. She lost interest in everything and refused to talk about it. She snapped at me whenever I said anything to her, and she didn't want to eat anything or to get out of bed. Basically, she just wanted me to leave her alone.

I didn't know what to do. It bothered me a lot that I was basically helpless when it came to helping her get through this. I was embarrassed about that because I felt that it was my responsibility as a man to take care of her. I was failing her when she needed me the most.

But truthfully, I didn't understand what I thought was an extreme reaction to the prospect of having surgery. She wasn't facing a terminal illness, nor was she looking at the loss of her fertility. She already went through menopause. There was a clear and easy path to ending her physical discomfort, and therefore, should have been readily accepted this course of treatment, or so I thought. The blinders I wore as a man prevented me from seeing my arrogance.

The surgery was scheduled to be performed in two weeks. I tried to call my mother to tell her about it, but she didn't answer her phone. I left her a message. She never called me back and there was no way that I was going to go looking for her. Even if I somehow managed to find out where she lived, there was no telling what I would have been walking into if I just showed up at her door – or how she would respond.

I would have called my Aunt Joyce too, but I heard that she had moved to Syracuse, and I didn't have a working phone number for her. I was hoping that my mother knew how to reach her. In the end, it might have been for the best that neither one of them were there because Mama was in no mood to put up with her crazy daughters and all of their drama. That went double for me.

I had her neighbor check in on her every day and I went to see her at least once a day. She just seemed so sad and lost. It was killing me, and I was beginning to get a little depressed myself.

"I want to go see her," Carla said calmly into the phone.

"Why?" I replied and cringed.

"I just do. It'll be alright. You'll see."

"But, as I said, she's not really up for visitors."

"I can go tomorrow at any time," she insisted.

"I don't think you understand how bad she is," I cautioned.

"What time can you pick me up?" she asked.

"Carla, I appreciate you wanting to help... I really do... but she's not..."

"What can it hurt?" she tendered. "You're not getting anywhere with her. You said so yourself. So, why not let me try."

"Well... I don't know..."

"Please... I want to. I know how much your grandmother means to you. You know you can trust me with her."

"I do trust you," I acknowledged.

"I know a little bit about depression," Carla offered. "That's all I'm say'n."

I held my breath a little and then slowly exhaled.

"Okay, if you really want to," I said and sighed heavily. "Thanks."

Mama had all the shades pulled down on the front windows and the whole place was dark. I turned on the lights in the front room and called out to her. When there was no answer, we walked down the hall to her bedroom door and knocked twice. At her quiet invitation, I opened the door and walked inside.

Mama was lying on her bed on her right side with the blankets pulled up to her neck. The room was illuminated only by a small nightlight plugged into the wall outlet.

"Mama, you okay?"

"Yeah, I'm good," she whispered.

"Do you want anything?"

"No," she answered.

"I brought someone here to see you," I offered.

"Who is it?" she asked under her breath.

Carla spoke right up, "Ms. Hicks, it's me, Carla. I have been worried about you, so I came to see you. I hope you don't mind."

There was no response.

"Would it be okay if I talked to you for a minute," Carla asked. "Please, I just want to make sure that you are okay."

Mama only nodded her head slightly. Carla moved passed me in one swift motion and gestured for me to leave. She closed the door behind me.

I stood there for a minute. I couldn't hear anything. I walked to the kitchen, turned on the light and immediately started clearing out the dishes that were in the sink. There was only a small pile. After that, I went into the bathroom and began cleaning that room as well and I took out the garbage. One thing about mama is that she always kept a clean house.

Over an hour later, I found myself sitting on the couch watching the evening news. I couldn't imagine what Carla was doing with Mama. I still couldn't hear anything- not a peep. Although I was more than a little anxious, I was also somewhat encouraged because this was a long time for Mama to be talking to anyone these days, so she was at least showing some signs of life. She had long ago made it clear that she had absolutely no interest in talking to me.

Carla finally opened the door.

"Uh, can you get some soup out of the refrigerator and warm it up," she directed. "Also, make some coffee please."

"Okay. Anything else?'

"No, that's it for now," she said and turned and went back into the bedroom.

I couldn't read her facial expression or the tone of her voice. I didn't sense any urgency in her demeanor. It was like she was asking for those things from a server in a restaurant. I jumped to my feet and went to the kitchen to get her what she requested.

I easily found the pot of homemade vegetable soup on the bottom shelf of the refrigerator and heated it up on the top of the stove. In addition to the soup and the coffee, I put some saltine crackers and a glass of water on the tray too. When I tapped lightly on the door, Carla opened it, and our eyes briefly met. She finally gave me a reassuring glance that immediately calmed my spirit.

Thirty minutes later, Carla walked out of the room with the tray. The only thing on it was the crackers and the empty soup bowl and utensils. She closed the bedroom door behind her.

"How'd it go?" I whispered.

She glanced back at the bedroom door and waved me off with her hand. I took the tray from her and walked into the kitchen. Carla followed closely behind. We were standing alone in the kitchen.

"Let me ask you something," she began. "Did this doctor explain to your grandmother exactly what a hysterectomy is?"

"Yes…I mean… I thought he did."

"Well, not according to her he didn't." she said while clearly trying to keep her voice down.

"He just told me about the tumors and how big they were and everything," I explained defensively. "He said that she needed this procedure because they weren't going to go away on their own and her pain was only going to get worse."

"But what about the actual surgery?" she questioned. "Did he tell you what he would be doing exactly?"

"No, he just said that the fibroids needed to come out and this was the standard procedure."

"Maybe it is or maybe it isn't," she attacked. "I'm not a doctor. But he is and if he is recommending this life changing procedure to a woman, then he should have made sure that she knew exactly what he was planning to do. That means that he should have sat his butt down on a chair next to her and explained everything that he is planning to do to her body in words that she is able to understand. He should have looked her in her eyes and answered every one of her questions and spent some time making her feel comfortable that this is the right decision for her."

"Um, you're right," I sheepishly agreed.

She looked both angry and annoyed, emotions that almost distorted her beautiful face- almost. My heart was beating fast in my chest, and I was overcome with a sense of guilt and shame.

"Sam, the thing is that this happens every day to us. Women, and particularly Black women, are treated like we are children and need for someone else to tell us what to do with our own bodies. These doctors talk down to us and make us feel like we are stupid or something. This is so maddening to me!"

I just looked her in the eye without saying a word.

"Did you know that your grandmother has never been to a gynecologist?" she pressed. "Poor thing… she thought that… it doesn't matter."

"How is she now?" I questioned.

"Better," she responded and tried to settle herself down. "I explained everything to her as best as I could. I think she gets it now. She might still have some questions, but at least now she knows that they are not going to turn her into …some kind of freak of nature."

"Well, thank you so much for doing that. I don't really know what to say."

"I'm just glad that you let me see her. You know that I wasn't really that sure about her at first, but now I see that she really is just the sweetest thing."

"Okay?" I questioned. "If you say so."

"No really," she insisted. "She has had a lot of trauma and disappointment in her life. She told me some of it. If you beat the puppy enough, it's going to stop coming to you when you call him. Your grandmother doesn't really trust people."

"I know."

"But you should know that she trusts you."

"Then I turn around and let her down too."

"It's not your fault. She knows that."

"I feel bad just the same."

"By the way, she doesn't want your mother to know about any of this."

"I haven't been able to get ahold of her anyway."

"Good. That's probably for the best."

"That's what I have been trying to tell you," I whined. "Now my mother, she really is a freak of nature."

"I know, you keep saying that. I'm starting to get the picture," Carla replied. "But won't she be angry when she finds out about the surgery. I mean, that's her mother. I would be mad if it were me."

"Yeah, she's gonna be out of her mind," I predicted. "But I'll let Mama deal with her daughter. She is really the only one who can. I literally refuse to go there with these people."

"I get that part, but what if something bad happens?" she countered. "I mean… I know that everything will be okay, but …on the chance that something goes wrong. Do you really want to take that chance?"

"I don't really see what choice I have, and I don't want to over think it," I contended. "I guess that I just have to take my chances and pray that nothing goes wrong."

Carla really was a miracle worker. Mama began her slow assent to normalcy right after their talk. Before we left her house, she came out of her room to greet me, and we spoke briefly. She looked okay. I couldn't tell if she had lost any weight after basically not eating for over a week. She said that she was going to take a bath. I was more than a little relieved.

Mama was nervous when we picked her up the morning of the surgery. I was too. Carla insisted on coming with us, so I had to stop by her place first. Mama had to be at the hospital at 5:00 am, but we were wide awake. Nobody said a word during the short ride there.

Carla and I sat in the waiting room while they prepped Mama. There was one other family there too. Who? I wasn't aware of how much I was fidgeting until Carla reached out and placed her hands on top of mine, which caused me to jump to attention. My eyes met her reassuring glance, and I told myself to calm down.

We were escorted to a small room where Mama was lying on her back on a gurney. She was awake and had her arm connected to a clear bag of fluid. She had a plastic cap on her head, and she looked like a little girl to me. We just tried to reassure her, and she said that she was good.

The surgeon walked in and made small talk with us. He seemed nice and made good eye contact with Mama. I double checked with her whether she had any questions. She said that she didn't have any. I only asked about the length of the surgery and when they would be starting.

When the time came, the nurse let us follow her to the operating room area.

"Okay, this is it," the nurse said. "You can say goodbye here and then you have to go to the waiting area. Someone will come out and talk to you when it is all over."

I walked to the head of the gurney, and I smiled at her while she tearfully looked up at me. I was shaking to my core, and I did my best to hide it. I placed my hand on her shoulder area, and I prayed aloud:

Father God, I know you to be an awesome God who can do anything but fail. And I also know that you are true to your word and anything that you have promised, you will do it for us. And I know that you are a healer and that Jesus bore our sickness and infirmities on the cross so that we don't have to try to do it alone. Father, I pray right now that your healing power will flow through my grandmother and that she will come out of this surgery like new. And we will declare that she is the healed of the Lord. Our hope is in you. We thank you for your grace and your tender mercies toward us. These things I pray in the name of Jesus. Amen.

When I opened my eyes, I saw that Mama still had her eyes closed and that

there were tears flowing from them covering the side of her cheeks and face. I could feel Carla pressed up next to me. She was also rubbing the middle of my back.

"Mama, we'll see you when you come out," I whispered. "It's all good."

She looked at me, but she didn't respond in any way that I saw.

Chapter 11

I woke up to a very chilly October morning. Although I hated winter, I was starting to dislike fall almost just as much because it foreshadowed that winter was coming. Typically, the rapid decline started right after Labor Day with colder nights that got progressively worse with every passing day. The next thing we knew there was a foot of snow on the ground and old man winter was angrily blowing bitter cold winds around with all the gusto that he could muster. As a child, I almost never had proper winter outerwear, which probably is the reason that I came to despise the cold so much.

Mama's surgery went well. She was scheduled to be discharged today, and I took the day off work to be with her. She had been in the hospital for four days and she was now demanding to go home. Her pain level was minimal, but she was still sore when she moved.

Mama had a seven-inch cut across her lower belly, which I hadn't expected her to show me, and which caused me to get a little lightheaded when she did. That's when it really hit me just how much of a violation this surgery really was. Fair to say that she wasn't a good patient, and everyone was glad to see her go home, especially the nurses.

We were still settling in at home when there was a knock at

the door. It was Carla and Kiana. I had no idea that Kiana was coming too. She had never met Mama before, and I wasn't sure that this was the right time for Mama to meet someone new.

They came bearing gifts of comfort foods, pillows and herbal teas and descended upon the wounded woman like sorority sisters. They pampered her and tended to her every need. I knew that Mama wasn't used to having people in her house or to this kind of attention, but she seemed to be taking to it just fine. Ultimately, they were a big help as Mama was already trying to do too much and fighting me on everything.

Miss Jenna from down the street already promised to come over every morning and make her breakfast and get her moving. The doctor said that he wanted her to get out of bed every day and walk around, which I didn't think would be a problem. I was more concerned about her trying to do too much. Carla gave Mama her telephone number and told Mama that she could reach out directly to her if she needed anything.

After we left Mama's house, the three of us had dinner at Carla's place. I went out and picked up Chinese food. After we finished eating, we watched the local news, and I listened to them dissect everything about the production. It was interesting.

Thereafter, we watched some show that I had never seen before. It was boring. Carla and I sat close together on the sofa, and I was starting to nod off. It was a good ending for what was a long day for me.

I volunteered to drive Kiana home when I left. She mostly just talked about people at the church. Obviously, I was glad that she was getting to know more people and feeling settled in and connected.

"Did I tell you that I am singing a solo in a couple of weeks?" Kiana asked at one point during the ride home.

"Yeah, I think you mentioned it."

"I asked Carla if she wanted to come hear me, but she said that she wasn't interested."

"Well, I don't think that she meant it that way," I pointed out. "She's just not ready to come to church now. It has nothing to do with you."

"I know," she conceded. "But what if she is never ready? Have you thought at all about that?"

"Not really. I guess we'll cross that bridge when we get to it."

"I think the Bible says, '*how can two walk together unless they agree?*'"

"True, but Carla and I will figure it out together. I really don't think that you have to worry about it."

"Oh, I know that honey," she retreated. "I'm just thinking out loud. I just love you both so much."

"Thank you, but we got this."

"Good, cause I only want what is best for the both of you. She told me that her counselor says that she still has a lot of healing to do from what happened to her when she was in high school. It makes me angry just thinking about how horrible that must have been for her. I can't even imagine how hard it must be for her. Who knows how long her recovery will take or if it even happens at all? At least we have our faith in God to get us through. Thank you, Jesus! She doesn't even have that."

I was only slightly annoyed, along with a growing uneasiness in my gut about Kiana. She had a knack for saying things that sounded innocuous, but which I seriously doubted were as virtuous as she tried to pretend. I had noticed that that wasn't something that she ever did when Carla was present. It was like she was assuming that the two of us shared a special relationship and we were morally superior to Carla because we served God and attended church together.

I called Carla after I got home just to say goodnight.

"Thank you again for all your help with Mama. I'm a little jealous that she listens to you and not to me."

"Oh, it's nothing."

"No, it's not nothing," I refuted. "It means a lot to me that you would put yourself out like that for her. I know that she hasn't always been the nicest to you."

"That's all water under the bridge," Carla asserted. "We didn't know each other. We are cool now. Women have a way of communicating that men don't get. It's way over your head so don't you worry your pretty little self over it."

"Is that right?" I reacted.

"Yes, you know it's true."

"If you say so."

"She laughed to herself."

"Hey, what made you bring Kiana with you?" I pivoted.

"She wanted to come," Carla explained. "I didn't think it would be a problem. I'm sorry, I probably should have asked you."

"No, it's not a problem," I fibbed. "I was just surprised to see her there, that's all. You never really know how Mama is going to react to people, especially if she's not feeling well."

"I think they got along," she reflected. "Your grandmother loved the chicken and dumplings Kiana made."

"I know," I replied. "It was nice of her to go through all that trouble."

"She said that your grandmother reminds her a lot of her aunt. I think that Kiana is doing a lot better now since she started going to your church."

"Well, everybody there seems to really like her," I said. "She's probably the best singer we got."

"She was a little homesick," Carla revealed. "This is her first time being away from Brooklyn and I think that she is finally starting to feel less like she's living on the far side of the moon."

"Good. I'm glad."

"And she has a lot of respect for you too," Carla added.

———•●•———

Kiana sang her solo beautifully. It was as if the Holy Spirit himself fell and moved freely among the entire congregation causing a holy hush. With tears streaming down her face, she sang, *I Exalt Thee*. It was powerful and the entire church was moved.

I only wished that Carla could have been there to witness it. Not as much to support her friend, but rather to just experience the real presence of the Almighty God- probably for the very first time. Although it was still all new to me, there was no denying that I was being completely made over. I desperately wanted that for Carla too.

Chapter 12

I looked forward to meeting with Hasan again, even though I didn't have good news. There was something about him that drew me to him. I knew that I had to be careful not to get too close. I gave myself a quick reminder as I was being escorted to the SHU. Ours was purely a professional relationship- nothing more.

"Sorry, but I don't have the best of news," I began as I looked across the table directly at him. "The district attorney's office is offering a plea to assault in the first degree with a sentence of 5 to 15 years."

His face showed no response, almost as if he hadn't heard me.

"Oh, you're right," he finally said. "That's not very good news."

I couldn't tell if he was just thinking about what I just said, or if he was just that disinterested.

"I don't mind telling you that I think that's outrageous," I offered. "But I'm not sure that I will be able to get them to come down."

"So, what are you telling me?" he asked.

"Going to trial is always a big gamble," I explained. "I looked at the video of the fight and it's hard to see how it started. All that is depicted there is a lot of commotion, which is out of frame.

There is no sound. It's basically worthless. The prison report, I think they call it an *"unusual incident report"* just talks about the three corrections officers responding to the fight and what they saw. They think the fight was about drugs."

"Drugs?" he questioned in disbelief. "That's a lie. I never used- ever. I don't have any drug violations since I've been incarcerated."

"I know."

"I was a pusher."

"I know that too," I conceded. "The problem is that there is not much I can do in terms of investigating any of this because it all happened in a prison. It's not like the real world. No one has to talk to us if they don't want to. As you predicted, none of the corrections officers called us back. Only one of them testified before the grand jury and he identified you as the one he saw with the homemade weapon."

"He never saw me with any weapon. I blocked the dude from coming at me with it."

"And he ended up with a stab wound in his chest that just missed his heart. That is going to get him some sympathy with a jury."

Hasan's eyes got big and then he stopped to rub them.

"I really don't know what happened myself," he explained. "I was sitting on the weight bench when I sensed him coming up from behind me. I turned and saw that he had the shank in his right hand, and I grabbed his wrist. I never touched the thing. I just pushed back at him, and I guess it went into his chest. The whole thing was probably less than ten seconds."

"And you still can't think of any reason why this guy would want to hurt you?"

"No, not at all. I never even spoke to him before. Somebody

put him up to it."

"Like who?"

"I already told you that I don't know that either. Someone has obviously got it in for me. There could be a thousand reasons."

"Well, what you are describing is classic self-defense," I concluded. "And this guy has already been convicted of physical assaults in the past."

"Will he have to testify?" Hasan wondered. "Because I don't think that he will."

"If you are asking me if you can be convicted if the alleged victim doesn't testify at trial, the answer is yes. But it's better for us if he doesn't testify. But they do have an eyewitness in the form of this CO Morgan."

"Oh, I didn't know that."

"But I can subpoena the victim and force him to testify, as long as he is physically able to do so."

"Good."

"So, what I'm hearing you say is that you don't want to take the plea deal," I summarized. "That you want to go to trial."

He raised an eyebrow and spoke, "You think I should take a plea?"

"No, at least not this one," I admitted. 'But I can't decide for you. It's your decision."

"Then no," he calmly stated. "No deal."

I was waiting for something more. I was used to clients showing a lot more emotion when I presented the prosecutor's first offer. Typically, there was a show of anger and righteous indignation. Most of the felons that I had represented were narcissists- either by design or by default. Clearly, Hasan was hardwired a little differently.

"Are you always like this?" I wondered.

"Like what?"

"So cool and composed?"

"*Self-control* is a fruit of the spirit," he said. "I have learned over time that God is very concerned about what we do with our bodies."

"What do you mean?"

"God wants to be glorified in everything that we do," he explained. "That means that we don't get to live the way other people live. When unbelievers look at us, they should see someone who isn't a slave to the flesh. When we show things like anger, greed, lust, and revenge, we are allowing the desires of our bodies to get the best of us. There is nothing godly about those things."

"I agree with that," I acknowledged. "So, you're telling me that you never get angry?"

"Nope, I'm not saying that."

"Cause in the end, we are still human," I maintained. "You can only fight against yourself for so long. Eventually something has got to give."

"True, we are all going to miss it sometimes. But that doesn't mean that we shouldn't be always striving to bring the flesh under submission to the Word of God."

"How does that work for someone in prison exactly," I boldly inquired. "If you don't mind me asking?"

"You mean because someone basically controls everything we do?"

"Yeah, I guess."

"You'd be surprised," he answered and laughed. "Wherever man is, there will be some immorality. It's even in the air we breathe. I don't mind telling you that I've seen some stuff here that I never would have been exposed to on the outside."

"Really?"

"Uh huh, everything from sex to … you know what I'm saying."

He looked at me hard and it made me a little uncomfortable.

"I see," I whispered.

"Yeah, but God is here too," he professed. "I found Jesus here in prison. An old catholic priest came to talk to us one night. He was this frail, white man whose voice trembled when he spoke. I'm not even sure why I went to the meeting in the first place. I guess I was just curious, you know. There was only about ten of us who showed up. But it was like every word he spoke bore a hole in my soul. I gave my old broken life to Jesus that night and he took it. Can you believe it? I had nothing else to give and he accepted it. That was over seven years ago, and I haven't looked back since."

"That's amazing!" I exclaimed.

"I've been locked up for ten years now," Hasan continued. "That's a long time. Everyone here knows that I'm a man of faith. I try to be a good example. That means keeping the rules, even the ones that don't make any sense."

"That's commendable, really," I said.

"Not everyone feels that way," he explained. "Keep in mind too that living upright is an offense to people who don't. I'm nobody's hero in here for sure. You can best believe that."

"You think that that's maybe why you were targeted?"

"Maybe... anything is possible."

"So, I'm curious," I presented. "When you pray what do you pray for? Safety and protection?"

"Hmm…mostly… for other believers, like Jesus did. And maybe for people here to be saved."

"For *you*?" I pressed. "What do you pray for yourself?"

"Probably to have faith like Paul."

"Really?" I replied. "Cause that's asking for a lot."

"I know it is."

"Paul was martyred," I stressed. "He was beheaded."

"Yes, I know."

"Oh."

———•●•———

The ADA knew that their offer to Hasan was high and so he wasn't too surprised when I told him in chambers that we rejected it. He just shrugged it off. While I understood that, as a practical matter, some of the crimes committed by incarcerated individuals needed to be prosecuted in the courts, I'm not sure that this was a good case for them to bring.

First, nobody really saw what happened and the victim was a known troublemaker. In the sworn statement he signed after the incident, he claimed that he didn't know who attacked him or why. This meant that the only witnesses against Hasan were correctional staff. There were a lot of facts here that worked to our advantage.

Secondly, in the end, the victim wasn't seriously injured. He was only in the hospital overnight and he didn't have any complications. The only follow-up treatment was wound care at the prison infirmary. Without more evidence of motive, the attempted murder charge was overreaching. Notwithstanding my obvious bias, this still wasn't one of the strongest cases for the prosecution.

However, Judge Spinoso was miffed for some reason that we didn't take the plea offer. I couldn't tell if he really thought the offer was fair or if he was just lazy and didn't want to preside over a week-long trial.

"Don't forget Mr. Hicks that this court frowns upon actions designed to delay justice," the judge said sternly with a scowl on his face.

"Good, then you should probably tell them that," I said and nodded toward the ADA. "It might help to move things along better."

"I'm not sure that I appreciate your tone Mr. Hicks," the judge snapped.

"My apologies, your honor," I said with a forced smile. "I just assumed that you were kidding."

We just stared at each other for what seemed like a good minute. Out of principle, I refused to retreat even an inch. Even if I lost the fight, I wasn't going down easy. Christians aren't supposed to be weak prey. Our God is mighty in battle!

As we were walking out of the courtroom together, the ADA, shook his head in amazement and turned to me and said, "Wow, I don't know what you did to him, but that judge doesn't like you very much."

"Doesn't matter, I don't like him back," was my flippant answer.

"So, how's that working for you?" he responded.

———— • ● • ————

I told Teresa about my interactions with Judge Spinoso. Mostly, I feared that the judge would come after me and make up lies about something I supposedly said or did. The whole office complained about how difficult he was -not just me - and how much we despised him. I was hoping to hear that she had our backs.

"I don't think that there is anything that I can do," Teresa said from behind her desk one afternoon.

"I'm telling you that this is bad," I presented. "He looks for opportunity to put down the people we represent. And with me, he makes everything personal."

"Maybe you should just try to limit your interactions with him."

"And just how am I supposed to do that," I balked. "He is the judge on most of my cases. Are you willing to reassign all of my cases I have with him?"

"You know that's not really possible."

"Then what?" I questioned.

"Maybe, you can just ignore him," she foolishly suggested. "I have known Vito and his wife for years. I'm telling you they are good people. I think that it's possible that the two of you just got off on the wrong foot for some reason."

"Yes, we did!" I asserted. "And we both know what the reason is!"

"You don't know that for certain," she insisted.

"Yes, I do!" I disputed. "I know a bigot when I see one. You can close your eyes to it if you want to. But I can't."

She looked startled. I wasn't exactly sure why. Her face turned a deep shade of red and she abruptly turned her head away from me.

"You're the public defender," I argued. "Most of the people we represent are Black. So, it's not just about me."

"Even if you're right, there is no way for you to prove it," she maintained.

"Everybody sees how he treats me and how he loves to tear down our clients."

"He's just going to say that you're the one in the wrong somehow and it's going to be your word against his," she insisted.

"There's nothing on the record. So, you will lose, probably more than you think, and bring the entire office down with you. Need I remind you, *he's the one wearing the black robe, not you!*"

Chapter 13

This was only my third time being at Carla's parent's beautiful home located in suburban Rochester, New York. It was thanksgiving and her whole family was there, including both of her siblings. Mama was annoyed at first that we weren't coming to her house for dinner, but I was able to convince her that it was still too soon for her to be on her feet that long doing all that cooking. She had dinner at Miss Jenna's house.

Although I was a little leery of Carla's father, who I found to be a little arrogant and hard to take at times, I was happy to go with her. And I liked her mother a lot. They just were different than most of the Black folks I knew.

Upon arrival, I was immediately banished to the den where all of the men were huddled around a huge television watching football.

"Hey Sam," Carla's father said as he stood to his feet and offered me his hand.

"Hey Chris, how are you?" I asked.

"Good man. Glad you could make it. Come let me introduce you. These are Carla's cousins from Chicago. That's Trevor, Big Mike, Brock, and Ray. Mike is married to Jackie's sister. Everyone, this is Sam. He's with Carla."

They all smiled and greeted me warmly.

"There are drinks and stuff in the corner," Chris pointed and said. "Otherwise, you know the drill. Make yourself at home."

"Thank you," I replied.

I remembered meeting a couple of them at Christina's and Eric's wedding last year. I walked over to the table and poured myself a cola. It looked like everyone else had a beer in their hand. Although I loved beer, I had pretty much given up alcohol since I got saved, except for an occasional glass of wine. I always knew that alcohol was a potential problem for me down the road. I sat down on one of the empty chairs that was available in the far corner and immediately directed my attention to the football game.

I was content to be a fly on the wall as I only had a passing interest in sports. The talk was mostly football. I gathered that all the cousins were Chicago Bears fans, and their team was losing to the Detroit Lions by three points in the second quarter. Based upon their reactions to every play, this was serious business.

Carla's brother, Christopher and Eric arrived shortly after me to a chorus of hellos.

"What's the score? Christopher asked.

"It's tied," Chris answered. "Y'all remember Eric?"

Eric sat down next to me. I wondered if it bothered him being the only white guy in the room.

"You like the bears too?" he whispered.

"No, I like the bills," I said.

"Me too," he replied and smiled. "They don't play today."

"You didn't have to work today?" I asked.

"Christina made me take it off. But I'm on call."

"Well, it's good to see you again. I haven't seen you since your wedding."

"Thank you," he replied. "Good to see you too. I feel like I know you through Christina."

"Same here."

Jackie, Carla's mother rushed in. She didn't look happy.

"Gentlemen, the agreement was that you could watch this game until halftime," she announced. "How much longer?"

"Maybe ten or fifteen more minutes," Chris said.

"Well, the food is done. Come eat as soon as it's halftime."

"Okay, mom," Christopher spoke. "We got it."

"Alright, just don't make me come back in here," she warned.

We all eventually gathered in the dining room and kitchen. There was plenty of food. I think all the women prepared it together. There were two turkeys and salmon for those who didn't eat meat. The desert table had about ten different items to choose from. Everything was delicious, but I still would have preferred my grandmother's Thanksgiving meal.

Carla pretty much left me alone, which I didn't mind. I wanted her to have a good time. I knew enough to stay out of any serious conversations, especially ones with her father. He was conservative, opinionated and liked to be heard.

"Sam, did you get enough to eat?" Jackie asked. I was standing in the doorway between the kitchen and the dining room.

"Yes, I did," I answered. "In fact, I'm stuffed. Everything was so good. Thank you."

"How's everything at work?"

"It's busy, but that's just the nature of the beast."

"Thank you again for not telling Carla about the time I visited you there," she whispered as she leaned into me. "I'm afraid that she would never forgive me."

"No problem," I responded. "I'm glad you came. It helped a lot."

"How's Carla really doing?" she wondered. "I ask her all the time, but she always gets so defensive. She gets that from her father."

My heart went out to her. I understood her frustration as someone who also cared deeply for her daughter and who was made to feel helpless. Carla preferred to suffer in silence and couldn't be trusted to timely cry out for help.

"I think she's good," I offered. "She likes her new position at the station. She is still going to counselling twice a week. We don't talk that much about that. I try not to pry- to give her space. But it seems to be helping. She has a full life, and she is balancing everything just fine."

"She does seem better to me," she stated and bit her lower lip in a way that reminded me of Carla. "I think that you are a big part of the reason for that."

"I think that you give me too much credit," I pushed back. "She's stronger than you might think. It's just a matter of not listening to the voices that try to keep her feeling bad and sad."

"Maybe, but I just feel better knowing that you are there watching over her."

"Thank you, but we're just a normal couple. We help each other get through."

"Well, I'm happy for the both of you."

"Thank you."

"Carla tells me that you are doing a lot with your church?"

"I'm still really new there, but I like it."

"You know, growing up my family was methodist," she offered. "I attended church a lot when I was a child. My mother insisted upon it. Chris and I decided to let our kids decide for themselves. We never pushed religion. I'm starting to think that that may have been a mistake. I see now that faith is important."

"Yes, it's definitely important to me now," I acknowledged. "It has changed the voices that I listen to in my own head."

She smiled to herself.

"I don't care what you say," she whispered. "You definitely are a good influence on my daughter from what I can see. For what it's worth, I'm rooting for the two of you!"

She rubbed the top of my shoulder.

"I know you are," I said.

"But I'm staying out of it," she articulated and quickly lifted both of her hands to the front of her face and threw her head to the side. "Far be it for me to have an opinion about the welfare of my children."

Right on cue, Carla approached and pressed herself close to me.

"I'm not sure that I like the looks of this," she said with a faint smile. "What are the two of you up to, I wonder?"

"Honey, it's nothing that serious I assure you," Carla's mom answered. "Sam was just telling me how much he likes his church."

"For some reason, it looked like more," Carla commented and took my hand. "But I need to steal my guy. Aunt Yogi wants to meet him."

Her family was great. Everyone had a good time just being together. I didn't hear one harsh word spoken throughout the afternoon, just harmless back and forth banter. That was simply unheard in my family, which had somehow perfected the art of *meanness* for sport.

However, Carla told me that she and Cristina and Christopher often resented what they considered to be meddling on the part of their mother. I guess it was a big thing for them growing up. However, speaking as one who never really had a mother or a father, I couldn't relate to even the idea of an overbearing parent.

Indeed, no one was ever really that focused on me or my so-called life. The truth is that I was often made to feel like I was invisible. Although I knew that my grandmother loved me, she wasn't always present emotionally. So, I didn't know fully what love felt like.

What I saw as I stood there among Carla's family was a room full of people who were united by blood and who loved each other. I was the only outsider present. Even Eric was family by marriage. This kind of unconditional love and support was the one thing I never ever allowed my heart to imagine because- down deep - I believed that it was nothing more than a pipe dream for me.

It was no wonder that I took to the church the way that I did. I always yearned to be a part of something bigger than me- something authentic. I just never considered the church before because, in my opinion, her light wasn't fully illuminated in the urban ghetto.

As one body in Christ, the church isn't just a place to learn about the Bible, but it's also a community of like-minded people who are invested in the personal and spiritual wellbeing of everyone there. I was only beginning to feel grounded and supported. I no longer hated myself.

Chapter 14

My mother finally returned my call. Lucky me. I wasn't home when she called, and she left a message on my answering machine. Although I'm ashamed to admit it, the angry tone of her voice initially caused me to panic slightly. I had to force myself to call her back.

"Sam, I stopped by Mama's house today and she told me that she had an operation *last month*?"

"Yes, about six weeks ago."

"How come nobody told *me*?" she complained.

"I called you and left you a message to call me."

"You didn't say nothing about no operation!"

"And you never called me back to find out why I was calling you."

"I think you should of made sure that I knew," she argued. "If someone was gonna be cutting on my mother then I needed to know."

"Why did you need to know?" I questioned. "That procedure was over a month ago. You haven't checked on her even once. Anything could have happened."

"Cause I didn't know."

"And six weeks is a long time," I stated.

"Cause I have stuff going on in my own life!" she erupted.

"You don't know what's going on with me. Everything doesn't have to be about you and Mama all the time. I swear, ya'll two get on my last nerves."

"Look, all I'm saying is that if you would have called me back like I asked you to, or called Mama yourself, then you would have known," I calmly stated. "Please don't try to blame me."

"Did I say that I blame you?" she provoked. "Did you hear me say those words? No, you didn't, so don't go and get yourself all hot and bothered about it honey. I mean really."

"That's what it sounds like to me," I protested.

"I'm just trying to find out what is going on!" she blasted. "That's all you gotta know."

"Mama is fine," I clarified. "She is recovering, and she is almost as good as new. If you saw her, then you know that's true. So, now you do know everything."

"No, I don't know everything, and it seems like you are trying to shut me out like you always do," she charged. "You don't always gotta act like you are so much smarter and better than everybody."

"Could we please just not do this?" I begged.

"Why did they need to cut on her in the first place?" Janet provoked. "She's an old lady now."

"She was having a lot of pain from tumors in her uterus."

"What kind of tumors?"

"They weren't cancerous, but they were big," I replied. "She just had some growths that needed to come out. She doesn't have that pain anymore."

"She never told me about any pain. How come this is the first that I'm hearing anything about this so-called pain?"

"Look, you should probably ask Mama that," I suggested. "She was embarrassed and didn't want anyone to know."

"That's why I'm asking you about it!" she persisted. "She's, my mother! I know she doesn't like to talk about that kind of stuff. I don't need you to tell me about my own mother."

"Apparently you do," I said. "You called me. Maybe you should check in with her more. She can speak for herself."

"And all I'm saying is that I don't appreciate you making all the decisions about her without checking with me," she came back. "You should have come found me. Utica ain't that big. You know where I stay at."

"I have no idea where you live," I maintained.

"You could have found me if you really wanted to!" she vented "Plenty of people know where I stay. You didn't even try to find me. And that's my point, you didn't want me to know!"

"That's ridiculous," I replied. "I'm not going to argue with you Janet. This doesn't make any sense."

"I'm just so sick and tired of you being Mr. Big Stuff," she fumed. "You just want everybody to think that you are so important and that you're so perfect all the time!"

"I can see where this is going," I said. "I'm sorry that you feel that way, but I'm a grown man and I don't have to listen to this anymore."

"Negro, I don't care nothing about you being grown…"

"I'm sorry," I interrupted. "I really do have to go so I'm hanging up the phone now. Have a good night, Janet."

I hung up the phone. My heart was beating fast in my chest, and I felt like I wanted to punch something- repeatedly. Mama used to say that talking to Janet made *you* stupid. It was in moments like this that I knew exactly what she meant... So much for a quiet evening at home.

———— • ● • ————

I was just getting ready for bed when the phone rang. I knew it was Carla before I answered. If we were going to talk at night, she usually initiated it because she called me from the station.

"I spoke to my mother today," I reported.

"Really? How did that go."

"Not good."

"She was angry about your grandmother?"

"Yes, that's an understatement."

"I thought so."

"She's always mad about something," I muttered. "So, why would this be any different."

"So, what's her story?" Carla wondered. "You never told me."

"*Story*?" I questioned.

"Everyone has a story."

"There isn't one," I asserted. "She's emotionally stunted like a feral cat- end of story."

"Sam!"

I laughed.

"Come on!" Carla urged. "Who was her person? Her father?"

"No, no father. Mama was never married."

"Your father then?"

"He was married, just not to her- just another loser she gave herself to indiscriminately."

"Promiscuity doesn't come easy to woman the way that it does to men," she maintained. "We aren't made that way."

"Well, she never seemed to have a problem spreading herself around," I reflected. "That's all I'm saying. She took to it like a drug."

"Maybe that's it," Carla speculated. "Maybe she has never had anyone to call her own."

"I have never known her to care about anyone except for herself," I said. "She lives on instinct - like a lot of the people I represent. So, in that way, she's not that different from a lot of people from Corn Hill."

"Have you ever asked her." Carla interrogated.

"Nope."

"Why not?"

"Cause I don't want to die," I joked.

"Sam, you should hear yourself. You're so hard on her."

"That's because she's hard on everybody else, especially me."

"Well, there's a story there," Carla insisted. "Her pain is real and probably runs deep. I feel sorry for her, and I've never met her."

"Okay, dear Abby," I replied. "Let's see if you feel the same way after that cat scratches one of your eyes out just because."

— • ● • —

I stopped by to see Mama. If my mother was there earlier in the week, then that meant that there was some drama. Obviously, Mama was more than capable of handling her, but I needed to make sure that she was okay just for my own peace of mind.

"How did you know she was here," Mama asked.

"Because she called me to complain about me not letting her know about the surgery."

"See, I told her not to bother you about that," Mama advised. "She don't ever listen to nobody. I told her that I didn't want people to know."

"She was fit to be tied."

"Well, that's yo mama for ya."

"I don't understand how she got like she is," I explored. "I mean, what's her problem really?"

"She was always too big for her britches," Mama disclosed. "Even as a child, she was hard-headed. I could never get either one of my daughters to mind good. They used to really embarrass me when I took them places. At least Joyce was a little scared of me, but Janet wanted what she wanted and was always throwing, what you call … *doldrums*."

"Tantrums," I corrected.

"Yea, there you go…When they were both little, they were always under me, but that all changed when they got bigger and decided that they knew more than me."

"Do you think that it had something to do with the fact that she didn't have a father?"

"You didn't have a father, even with her as a mama, and look how good you turned out."

"I just have never been able to figure her out," I said.

"There is such a thing as a bad seed," she pointed out. "It won't grow no matter what you do to it."

"You never look back and wonder about them?"

Suddenly a pained look appeared on her face. Before that, I thought she was mostly being defensive, which made sense to me.

"Um, I used to feel really bad about them," she revealed. "But both of their daddies were good- for- nothing- scoundrels, and they turned out just like their daddy."

"I get it, but I just feel bad sometimes," I admitted. "I wish that things could have been different between us."

"Sam, you really are good-hearted, but you have to get over

some things when it comes to Janet," she opined. "It ain't your fault - none of it! You can't make people be who they ain't!"

"So, you think that I should just accept her the way that she is?"

"Uh huh, that is surely how I see it," she maintained. "Cause what else you gonna do?"

"I don't know," I admitted.

"You best let that woman be crazy and go about your business!" Mama warned.

Chapter 15

Kiana called me just as I was getting home from work. She sounded upset. She said that her bathroom sink was leaking, and she couldn't turn off the water. I dropped everything and hurried over to her place.

When she opened the door, she was wearing a black terrycloth robe that went down to her knees. She quickly waved for me to come in and closed the door behind me. Her hair was tied up and she was barefoot. I thought she looked different somehow.

Her apartment was neat and clean. It smelled like she was cooking something. She led me through the living room to a small bathroom. The two doors under the vanity were wide open and all the products that she normally kept there had been taken out and moved into a corner. The floor was only a little wet in spots. I had expected worse.

Wisely, she had strategically placed several towels on the floor. There was a big black pot under the sink catching the steady drip of water coming from the pipe. I climbed underneath and I only had to apply medium force to turn the valve that turned off the water.

I almost hit my head on the bottom of the sink trying to get to my feet.

"Oh, watch out!" she exclaimed.

"No, it's alright. I'm good."

"Oh, thank you so much, Sam," she said and handed me a small hand towel. "I don't know what I would have done without you."

"You're welcome."

"I called the landlord, but he just said to turn the water off under the sink," she advised. "I tried, but I wasn't strong enough to turn that thing."

"I know. Sometimes the valve gets rusted on."

"Such a relief," she voiced. "Thanks so much."

"It's nothing, really," I replied. "Glad I could help. I'm not really that handy around the house."

She led me out of the bathroom.

"Can I get you anything, Sam?"

"No, thank you. I'm good."

"How about a little dinner before you leave?" she solicited. "I made beef stew. There's plenty."

"Thank you, but I can't."

"C'mon, please," she begged. "You're always buying me brunch. This is my chance to pay you back a little."

"I appreciate it Kiana, but I have a busy day tomorrow and I still have work to do tonight."

"But you have to eat," she pointed out. "It won't take long. Everything is already done."

"Hmm…"

"C'mon, pretty please?"

"Okay," I reluctantly agreed. "If you're sure that it's no trouble."

"No trouble at all," Kiana replied. "Just have a seat there. I promise, it will only take a minute."

I was a little uncomfortable being in her space. She turned on some soft worship music, which caught me off guard. Although I listened to music in the car, I rarely played any kind of music at home. Neither did Carla.

"Sam, what would you like to drink?" she called out from the kitchen. "I have wine."

"No wine. Water is good."

"Okay. It will just be another minute."

She turned and walked down the hall. When she returned, I could see that she had changed out of her robe. She was now wearing a full-length, tight-fitting, short-sleeved print dress. She was still barefoot.

"Come have a seat."

"Everything looks good." I said.

"Thank you. Can you bless the table?"

Again, I was caught off guard, but I managed to stumble my way through saying grace.

"So, how was your day dear?" she asked as she passed me the salad dressing.

"Very funny," I said.

She giggled.

"How is your grandmother doing?"

"She's good. Just glad to get this thing behind us."

"I just love her. She's so funny."

"Yup, she's a laugh a minute," I played along.

"You're so good with her," she asserted. "She's really lucky to have you."

"Thank you for saying that."

"You never cease to surprise me," she said.

She gave me a prying stare that I chose to ignore.

"How so?" I inquired.

"No, I just meant that you're a rare kind of guy," she complimented. "I'm not sure that I have ever met anyone quite like you before."

"I don't know what you mean."

I swallowed a spoonful of stew, which was delicious.

"It's just that it seems like Black men always leave, one way or another."

"Because that's pretty much all we know," I volunteered.

"So, what makes you so different?" she prodded. "I really want to know."

"I'm not sure that I really am that different," I acknowledged.

"You're just being modest," she concluded.

"Not really. God saved me from myself long before I knew he even could. I deserve none of the credit."

"Is it hard representing people you know are guilty?" she pivoted.

"Who am I to judge?" I asked and shrugged.

"That's a good way of looking at it."

"The thing I hate the most is that these young boys can't seem to stop shooting each other."

"One of my cousins was killed like two years ago," she disclosed. "He was just 19 years old."

"I'm sorry to hear that… I'm just saying that I have more in common with these guys than I might care to admit. I certainly have some of the same weaknesses. It's only by the grace of God that I was able to make some different choices."

"I think that's nice," she commented. "You're very humble."

She was looking at me oddly again,

"Not really," I said. "I just don't kid myself about who I am."

"That's a gift in itself in my opinion," she stated. "We all are kidding ourselves about something- some just more than others.

"Maybe."

"Tell me this, Mr. Hicks," she shifted again. "What do you look for in a woman?"

She looked at me intently.

"I don't know what you mean," I resisted. "I have Carla."

"But if she was out of the picture for some reason, what would you be looking for?"

"Why would she be out of the picture?"

"I don't know," she equivocated. "Things happen."

"Like what?"

She hesitated briefly. I could see her thinking.

"Um…I'm just asking what a professional Christian man, such as yourself, look for in a woman?"

"Oh…ah…I'm not sure that I know myself… I just know it when I see it."

"Is it a physical look?"

"Not entirely," I resisted. "I know why you would think that, but there are plenty of attractive woman in the world. They're literally everywhere."

"Then what?" she prodded. "You mean like a soul mate kinda thing?"

"Maybe… er partly…I don't know," I wavered. "I don't know how to explain it. Obviously, Carla is a very beautiful woman. But there is also something about her that calms the storm in me."

"Calms you?"

"Before her I was kinda lost in space and time."

We just looked at each other in silence for a few seconds.

"So, you're a poet too," she finally said.

"Hardly," I answered and turned away. I was embarrassed by my show of vulnerability.

"You can never see yourself with anyone else?" Kiana pursued. "Is that what you're saying?"

"I used to think that no one is irreplaceable." I divulged. "But now, I'm just not so sure. That's certainly not true for God who we can't possibly live without. So, I don't know why it would be true for the people who he has intentionally placed in our lives."

"I don't know about that either," she added. "All I know is that I want a man of my own, even if it's not real …or make believe."

"You can't mean that," I uttered. "Excuse me for saying, but that sounds a little desperate."

"I know how it sounds," she stated emphatically.

"I think you deserve better."

"Me too," she whispered.

There was a cold intensity in her eyes that wasn't there a few moments ago. It reminded me a little of something I had seen once before in the eyes of an evil client. I had a sick feeling in the pit of my gut, and I forced myself to come up with something- anything- different to talk about. I just wanted to go home.

I didn't say much after that. She hastily regrouped. She talked about her family and her life in Brooklyn, and she managed to get me to laugh a few times. I turned down her offer for coffee and made my quick exit as gracefully as I could.

"Thank you for dinner," I said from just inside her front door, facing her directly.

She smiled warmly.

"You're welcome," she reciprocated. "I appreciate you helping me with my sink."

"No problem."

"Maybe we can do it again sometime," she said and smiled.

"Maybe."

"So, I guess I'll see you on Sunday."

"Sure thing," I replied.

She suddenly leaned into me to kiss me. I deftly turned my head just in time and her lips landed mostly on my left cheek.

"Goodnight," she whispered.

"Goodnight."

— • ● • —

Obviously, I told Carla that I had dinner at Kiana's house. Otherwise, I had no intention of ever talking about that evening again. I didn't really say much else because I didn't know what to say about it. Her feeble attempt to seduce me, if that's what that was, truly was pathetic. For some unknown reason, I felt like I had done something wrong.

"I told her that she needed to get her sink fixed over a month ago," Carla revealed.

"Why didn't she do it?"

"I'm not sure. She said she was going to call her landlord. I just assumed that she had already taken care of it."

"Well, she doesn't really have a choice now," I said. "She can't use it at all now."

"Is that the first time that you tried her food?" she asked. "I told you she's an excellent cook."

"Yeah, the stew was great."

Chapter 16

My grandmother was having some pelvic pain from the scaring. Mama called Carla, who in turn reached out to her sister Christina and Eric. They said that this was a known side effect of a hysterectomy, and it was probably nothing serious. But they also advised that Mama needed to be seen by her doctor as soon as possible.

Carla took her to the appointment. I met them at Mama's house after they were through at the doctor's office. I brought Mexican food, which I knew Mama loved. Fortunately, the doctor wasn't too concerned. There was no sign of infection and better wound care was recommended, including continued use of silicone gels to moisturize the area. She was improving. The doctor said that it usually took about a year or so for scar tissue to mature on its own.

I asked Mama again if she wanted me to call Janet. She was adamant that she still didn't want her daughter involved. She complained that she had only seen Janet once since the surgery, and that she only called once.

"She only called me because she wanted to know if I was making a Germain chocolate cake for thanksgiving," Mama adduced.

Frankly, I was relieved as I wasn't ready for another go

around with Janet Hicks. It took me a couple of days to get over our last encounter. The thing is I had been caught in the middle of the two of them since the day I was born. Something had to give.

But I was very pleased with the way that Mama's relationship with Carla was progressing. Mama clearly trusted Carla and needed something from her that she couldn't get from me. I certainly had no desire to know every detail of her medical situation considering her desire for privacy. Ultimately, she didn't seem to be jealous of Carla anymore and I was thrilled about that.

— • ● • —

Carla and Kiana went Christmas shopping in New York City. Carla was very excited about their midweek excursion downstate. Utica was too small for her. She liked the bright lights and culture that one generally finds only in bigger cities. I could see this potentially becoming a problem for us down the road because I had absolutely no desire to live in a big city and it was only a matter of time before she got a job offer in a larger market.

She called me twice from Brooklyn. First, she wanted to know Mama's shoe size. Then she wanted to know if I thought that a Buffalo Bills vintage baseball cap was a good gift for her dad. I could hear the excitement in her voice. I was glad she was having a good time.

We spoke late Thursday night on the phone after they got home. Apparently, something odd happened involving Kiana when they were somewhere near Time Square.

"I was standing with Kiana on the sidewalk and this guy came up to me and handed me a bouquet of flowers," she recounted.

"Flowers?" I questioned.

"Yeah, he just came up to me and said that he wanted me to

have them because he thought I was beautiful. Then he just walked away."

"You took them?"

"Yes, I did," she said. "I didn't know what else to do and it happened so fast."

"What did he look like," I inquired.

"Like a normal guy. Why?"

"If I got in a fight with this guy, who do you think would win, me or him?"

"What?"

"I wanna know if you think I could take this guy cause I don't appreciate him putting the moves on my woman."

"He did no such thing," she resisted.

"I'll be the judge of that."

"Can you be serious for just a minute please?" she demanded.

"I am being serious," I said.

"No, you're not."

"What were you wearing?" I continued.

"Cut it out!" she lashed out. "I'm done with you already. I'm trying to tell you something and you keep fooling around."

"Okay, okay I'm sorry," I apologized. "What happened after the crazy guy gave you his cheap flowers?"

"I didn't say he was crazy."

"I thought that was a given."

"Never mind," she cried out in despair. "I don't know why I even try with you."

"Okay," I laughed and relented. "I'm sorry... go ahead, tell me... please. I want to hear it."

"I thought what he did was cute," she insisted. "...But Kiana clearly didn't. She immediately shut down,"

"Shut down how?"

"She just seemed bothered and sulked all afternoon like a teenager," Carla said. "It was… disturbing."

"Did you ask her what was going on?" I probed.

"She said it was nothing, but I have never seen anything quite like it before," she reflected. "It was like night and day…almost like something, or someone took over her body and she disappeared for a couple of hours."

"She probably was just jealous," I opined.

"*Jealous*?" she questioned.

"Yeah, this guy chose you to fawn over, and she was standing right there."

"We didn't even know him," Carla protested.

"Doesn't matter." I asserted. "The green-eyed monster got the best of her."

"Now that's really silly!" she rejected.

"That's what all the cheerleaders say."

"How'd you know I was a cheerleader?"

"I saw the picture at your parent's house."

"Oh yeah, I forgot about that picture," she said.

"Hey, do you still have that uniform?" I flirted.

She ignored me. "I just thought Kiana was having a bad moment, you know she got annoyed about something."

"She did," I maintained. "She was annoyed about *you*. I mean, do you really have to have all the boys?"

"I only have the one," she came back. "And he's really getting on my nerves right about now."

— • ● • —

We had a wonderful Christmas together! Mama insisted that we come to dinner at her house on Christmas Eve. I was worried that she might overdo it, but she didn't show any signs of being hampered in any way. She made all the foods I loved growing up, including her cakes, which were well known throughout Corn Hill.

The thought occurred to me that my mother could pop in at any moment, but fortunately, she never did. Carla unashamedly continued with her shallow scheme to bribe Mama by buying her several gifts. I don't remember my grandmother getting too many gifts over the years from anyone other than me, so she was very excited and made a big fuss about everything.

The plan was that we would spend the early part of Christmas day alone at her place and then go to Rochester in the early afternoon. We slept in and cuddled together and exchanged gifts over breakfast. I got Carla a gold teardrop diamond bracelet and some cookbooks. Carla got me a black cashmere overcoat and a black leather briefcase. I never knew she hated my old one.

Christmas with the Jenkins family was a much smaller affair than Thanksgiving had been. There was only seven of us. Christina and Eric were already there when we arrived. Christopher came later by himself. Carla once told me that her brother was a bit of a playboy, and their mother never liked any of the women he dated.

We mostly just ate and sat around in the kitchen and dining area. There was a lot of talk about fashion as the women gifted each other with the latest, greatest garments and footwear. I always felt that Carla was more like her mother than she cared to admit.

The guys all ended up in the den watching sports again. I was pressured into having a beer, which I just nursed. Eventually Eric got a call and had to leave, and Christopher disappeared somewhere, leaving me alone with Carla's dad.

"Can I get you something, Sam?"

"No, thanks. I'm good."

"I'm glad that we're alone," he said. "I've been meaning to talk to you about something."

"Sure," I said. I was only a little anxious.

"I was just wondering man how it's going with you and Carla? Jackie's already got the two of you married and moving in across the street with the grandchildren."

I laughed. "We're doing good I think."

"You think?"

He suddenly looked very serious.

"I just meant that I know what I think," I tried to explain. "Obviously, I can't speak for Carla. You'd have to ask her yourself."

"That's the thing, that's one hard nut to crack," he reflected.

"I know she is."

"I can still remember the day she was born like it was yesterday," he offered. "We already had Christopher, and he was great and everything, but I'm telling you Carla was the most beautiful baby that I had ever seen. She was perfect in every way."

"Really?"

"The first month after she was born, I used to sneak into the nursery in the middle of the night just to watch her sleep. Jackie caught me a couple of times. She thought I was losing it. I did too. I was so in love with this baby that I didn't know what to do. The feeling inside was an irresistible force."

"Wow!" I exclaimed.

"We have always been close, me and Carla. But that changes over time. When you have a daughter of your own you will know what I mean. They still want you there, but suddenly they insist that you back up. And you really don't have a choice."

He was deep in thought. I could see it in his eyes. I saw

sadness there too, a lot of it. For some reason, I was very surprised to see it.

"And then when … what happened to her… you know… what that kid did to my baby… it was like…like I fell off a deep cliff and died." he articulated. "I was filled with every emotion known to man and they were all running through my veins like crack cocaine."

My throat was suddenly very dry, and I felt my eyes watering. I dabbed at them with my middle two fingers because I didn't want him to see that I was crying. I took a big sip of my warm beer and cleared my throat a couple of times. I don't think he saw.

"I simply didn't know what to do," he divulged. "It was like I was frozen in time. Jackie took the lead, and I just had to let her. She dealt with that boy's family and Carla and the doctors, and I really wasn't even there. I knew that if I allowed myself to feel the full force of this thing, that there was no telling what I would do."

"I get it," I forced myself to say.

"I'm just being honest with you," he explained. "I felt like less than a man. It really messed with my psyche."

"What happened wasn't your fault," I sympathized.

"Yes, it was!" he came back strong. "I let my baby down. If something like this would have happened under my father's watch, he would have handled it like a champ."

"You did the best you could," I argued. "Bad things happen to all of us."

"I know but…"

"Only God is all powerful and all knowing," I interrupted. "It's arrogance and prideful to pretend that we are like him."

"*Arrogance?*" he questioned and distorted his face slightly.

"There are plenty of things that we do that really are our fault," I boldly spoke. "So, don't accept the blame for things that aren't rightfully yours. It's a lie that can cripple even a strong man."

He just stared at me, and his pain was contagious. But it wasn't mine to have and I was only willing to temporarily hold a piece of it. He never shed a tear and so mine seemed out of place. I was only slightly embarrassed.

"Okay but is she going to be okay?" he asked in a voice that had an almost child-like innocence. "Just tell me that because I can't handle too much more."

I let the question hang in the air momentarily out of fear of saying the wrong thing. It was saturated with years of guilt and shame, so it was stifling.

"If she really wants to be," I heard myself say. "She has a lot going for her, including a father who loves her with his whole heart."

Startled, he flinched like he was stung by a bee before slouching over in his seat. Then he put his head down. He finally cried.

Carla's mom insisted that we stay Christmas night at their house because of the report of snow on the roads. I slept in the guest room, which had its own bathroom and was nicer than my whole apartment. We left right after breakfast.

"Can I talk to you about something?" I asked at one point on the drive home.

"What is it?"

"Did you know that Kiana gave me a Christmas present?"

"No, what was it?"

"It was a leather Bible with my name engraved on it?"

"Oh, that's nice," she said.

"Well not really," I spoke. "Nothing against her, but I don't want her buying me presents. It makes me feel uncomfortable."

"I think she is just grateful that you got her connected with your church. I know she really likes it. You came over and helped her with her sink. The gift is just a goodwill gesture."

"You don't think it's like…intrusive or something?"

"It's just a Bible, Sam, of all things. It's not like she bought you underwear or something."

"You told her what kind of underwear I wear?" I teased.

"Don't be silly," she said in a huff. "Why would I tell her that?"

"I don't know, maybe you were having some kind of little joke at my expense. You better not be telling people about me in my boxers. That's supposed to be a secret."

"I just think you have a hard time in general with people giving you things," she posed. "I know how you guys are."

"I don't think that's true," I disputed. "It's just that she's so …I don't know… weird about everything."

"My parents got you presents. Do you feel the same way about them giving you gifts?"

"No, of course not," I replied. "But since you brought it up, I think you're the one who told them to get me new clothes because you are trying to do a make-over on me."

"A make-over?"

"That's right. I read about it in my men's magazine. You are trying to put your mark on me like I'm some kind of piece of meat and I'll have you know that I'll have none of that young lady!"

She chuckled. "Sam, besides your work clothes, you only have like two shirts and one pair of jeans."

"Ah ha!" I reacted. "So, you admit it! You're a schemer! Finally, we're getting somewhere!"

"Look, my mother asked me what you would like, and I made a few suggestions…like you did with Christina and the bracelet!"

"What!" I exclaimed. "She told you!"

"I knew it all along," she claimed and put her hands over her mouth while she convulsed with laughter. "Don't get me wrong. it's a great gift – too good! There's no way you picked it out by yourself."

"I feel betrayed, and I'm done with all of you."

"Oh, get over yourself, Sam. You're such a big baby."

"Your words are hurtful to me," I blabbered. "Please don't speak to me ever again."

"But seriously, about Kiana, I hear you." she circled back. "I'll mention it to her."

"Okay, thanks. I appreciate it."

— • ● • —

Carla and I had a quiet New Year's Eve celebration. It was too cold to really go anywhere. We stayed in, had a quiet dinner and I was fast asleep by 1:00 am.

There was a message from my sister Tasha on my answering machine when I got home on New Year's Day. I immediately called her back at the number she left.

"Happy New Year, Sam," Tasha said.

"Same to you. How are you?"

"I'm good. It's been a minute."

"Yes, it has."

"How's Mama?" she wondered.

"She's good. She had surgery a couple a months ago, but she's fine now."

"What kind of surgery"
"A hysterectomy."

"A what? I didn't even know someone her age could have one

of those."

'Me either."

"How's   Janet?"
"I haven't really seen her in a while?"

"I heard that she has a 'girlfriend' … like a *girl* who is more than a friend, if you know what I mean."

"Yup, I met her," I replied. "Mama did too and I'm sure you can guess how that went. But I don't think they are together anymore."

"I see that our mother is still a trip."

"Hardcore to the bone," I said.

"I know that's right," she expressed. "That's one of the reasons that I'm so glad that I left Utica - not that Buffalo is that much better. Just a different kind of drama."

"How's Tonya?"

"Ah, she's good too. She lives around the corner from me with her three kids. I see them a lot cause she works midnights doing security at the hospital and I babysit for her."

"Well tell her that I said hi," I said. "You guys should really come see Mama sometimes and bring the kids. I'm sure that she would like to see her great grandchildren."

"I know, we gotta do that. Our kids only know one side of the family."

"What side is that?" I asked.

"We got two sisters and two brothers on our father's side who live here in Buffalo."

"Oh, I didn't know that."

"Yeah, that's kind of how we got here in the first place from Rochester."

"Well, I'm glad that you guys have some family that is close by," I stated.

"But Sam, I just want you to know that we are still family too. Me, you, and Tanya will always be connected. I know that we don't have contact like we should, but we still have some of the same blood through our mother. We grew up in the same house."

"I haven't forgotten," I said.

"You have nieces and nephews too who you don't even know," she remarked. "You would like them. My two are smart like you. I don't know about those other ones."

I chuckled.

"Maybe I will meet them all one day," I expressed. "Just keep them away from Janet."

"Um…about her…Sam, I always wanted to tell you something because I don't think you know."

"What's that?" I solicited.

"I don't even know if I should be telling you this now… but I think that you have a right to know," she wavered. "I just don't want you to be mad at anybody."

"I won't get mad."

"Are you sure?"

"Yes, I'm sure," I replied. "We're not kids anymore Tasha. You can tell me anything."

"Your father raped Janet," she slowly articulated. "That's how she got pregnant."

"What?"

"They weren't having an affair," Tasha explained. "He was like 40 years old or something, and she was just a teenager. Mama was the one who was dating him."

"Who told you this?" I asked calmly.

"Hard to say," she advised. "I think me, and Tonya always knew. A lot of people in Corn Hill know. Mama just didn't want you to know."

"Why?"

"You became *her* baby. That's why she loves you so much."

"I see."

"I think Janet and Mama kinda blamed each other for what happened, and they have been wrestling with each other ever since."

"With me in the middle," I stated.

"…Right."

"And nobody ever told me."

"I know," she replied.

"Well, okay then," I mouthed.

"Are you mad?" Tasha questioned.

"No, I'm not mad," I lied.

"I'm really sorry, Sam."

"It's ancient history at this point, right?" I heard myself say. "I wouldn't know my father if I tripped over him."

"I know, but I just don't want you to feel bad," she expressed.

"I appreciate that," I said. "I mean it."

"Like I said, I just think that you have a right to know - even after all of this time."

I just wanted to get off the phone at that point. She changed the subject and began catching me up on the things that have transpired in her life since we last connected well over a year ago. I listened politely, although nothing was registering with me.

I kept thinking, *I am the spawn of a rapist and a pedophile.*

Suddenly, I was reminded of what Carla's dad said about having mixed emotions running wild through his body like a narcotic drug. I was paralyzed by my shock, hurt and anger. I never really knew who I was before, and I felt alone in the world for so long. By the time I hung up the phone with Tasha, I was trauma stricken.

I didn't feel like facing people, so I called into work the next morning. I was having a hard time settling down and I had only dozed off and on throughout the night. I felt drained and hung over. Rather than toss and turn in bed, I lay on the couch in front of the television all day and felt sorry for myself.

Carla called me at 10:30 pm. I rushed to the phone like a newborn baby to the breast. I immediately latched on and told her everything.

"Wow, Sam, that's amazing!" she finally said.

"I know."

"What are you going to do?"

"What can I do?" I reasoned. "What's done is done."

"Are you going to talk to your grandmother?"

"And say what?" I posed. "I know that you've been lying to me for all these years."

I felt a rush of emotion once again.

"Well yes…maybe," she considered. "What she did wasn't right. She should have told you. She knew all this time why your mother was mistreating you. They all knew."

"Probably laughing behind my back."

"I don't think anybody was laughing at you," Carla contended.

"I'm not so sure," I resisted. "Tasha said that a lot of people in Corn Hill know about it."

"What's there to laugh about?" she asked. "It's all so sad. You grew up in a house full of pain and resentment."

"Filled to the brim."

"And I have to say that I for one really feel for your teenage mother who obviously went through some real trauma without any real support from anyone, including from her own mother. At least I had support from my family and still it was really hard."

"I know."

"I don't know how she did it," Carla added.

"Mostly by taking it out on me."

"I'm sorry, Sam."

"It's a lot, I know," I said with a heavy sigh. "I don't know what to think."

"That just means that there's a lot to forgive," she said. "Every family has stuff."

"I don't know if I can forgive them though," I admitted. "I don't want to."

"You at least know that you should forgive them," she encouraged. "Don't do it for them; do it for you. Free yourself."

"Just like that?" I questioned. "Just pretend like my entire childhood never happened."

"You don't have to do it today. Give it a little time."

"*Forgiveness*," I spoke aloud. Just the sound of the word vibrated in my head like a bell.

"You always knew that your grandmother is broken," she said. "But you also know that she loves you. And you love her. I remembered how you prayed for her before her surgery. I had never seen anybody do that before. I wish that somebody prayed for me like that."

"What do you mean?"

"I just mean that it was really beautiful."

"No, I mean, I pray for you every morning when I wake up because you are usually the first thought that enters my mind."

I heard her gasp.

"You mean you didn't know?" I asked matter-of-factly.

"No, I didn't," she whispered.

"I'm sorry, that's on me," I apologized. "I thought you knew. You mean the world to me, and I plan to cover you in prayer every day for the rest of my life if you let me."

She was quiet.

"You there?" I asked "Hello?"

"Sam …I don't know what to say… You're making me emotional."

"You don't have to say anything. It's true."

"I know it is," she acknowledged. "You have such an amazing capacity to love."

"Look where it got me," I whined. "My grandmother betrayed me, along with everyone else in our house."

"I'm not so sure about that," she countered. "You still don't have all the facts."

"I don't want to hear any more *facts*. I can't…"

"But where would you be without her?" she prodded.

I knew where she was going with this, and I didn't want to answer her.

"Where?" she repeated.

"Probably dead and buried someplace," I spoke solemnly.

"You should probably hold on to that thought and start there."

I sighed heavily.

"Sam, you're a survivor," she encouraged. "You really are! That's one of the things that I love most about you. Nobody is as fearless as you!"

I hesitated, "I don't know."

"Yes, you do!" she pressed. "Think of it as the last piece of the puzzle that you need in order to see yourself clearly. Aren't you ready for that? Isn't this what you have always wanted? To know the truth?"

"Yes, I guess it is," I admitted mostly to myself.

"What made your sister call you in the first place and tell you this now after all this time?"

"I'm not sure. She didn't say."

"Sounds to me like your prayers have been answered," she wisely pointed out.

"You're right," I reluctantly conceded. "About all of it… Thank you."

"You're welcome," she replied. "You know you could have called me when you first found out. I'm sure that it was quite a shock to you. I know how you stew over things."

"I didn't want to bother you."

"You're my man!" she exhorted. "You're not a bother…most of the time."

"Excuse me?"

She laughed.

I was much better after my conversation with Carla, and I knew that I would be able to sleep again. Like I told Kiana, Carla calms my storms.

The fact that I was becoming more dependent upon her for emotional support was both a blessing and a trial. While it felt good to have someone who I could lean and depend on, doing so didn't come naturally to me and a small part of me fought against it – a defense mechanism, I think.

Even though I had only been a true believer in the living God for a short time, I fully understood that it would have been a huge mistake- and a giant step backward- to see myself as a victim again. Rather, it was time for me to lean into my new identity. Free people act and think like they are free!

I was finally winning in my struggle with the feelings of inferiority that had a stranglehold on me most of my life. So, I was determined to not let this new information about the deviant who sired me, and all the rest of it, undermine the undeniable truth that God loved me, even though I hadn't exactly felt loved for most of my life.

Although I didn't have any idea what to do about my grandmother - or about my mother - I completely accepted that I needed to stay on the path that I had charted for myself. I knew in my heart that I was moving in the right direction as I pursued God and grew in faith. Carla was right, I wasn't afraid. And I wasn't weak either.

———•●•———

Mama told me that Janet paid her a visit on New Year's Day. She said that Janet only came "to eat up my food." In the past, I just took everything Mama said about Janet at face value because it was easy for me to stand with her in judgment of the person who I believed had failed me the most in life. However, hearing the negativity from Mama now made me uncomfortable. I realized that I had never heard her say one thing nice about Janet- ever. And I knew firsthand what it feels like to be rejected by your mother, something that usually doesn't happen even in the wild.

Chapter 17

Typically, the public defender's office can only represent one of the defendants in a case at a time. This meant that in cases where more than one person was arrested stemming from the same criminal activity, we only represented one of them and the other defendants were assigned private attorneys from outside law firms. Most of these law firms, who were paid next to nothing by the county, treated the assignment by the court as necessary public service and sent their younger, inexperienced attorneys to handle these matters in court.

I was in court this morning waiting for my two cases to be called. The case before mine was being defended by John Roberts, a young, good-looking attorney from one of the local firms. He was about 25 years old with blond hair and blue eyes. I had only spoken to him a couple of times, but he seemed like a nice guy.

John was standing behind the podium with a young Black teenager who was being arraigned on a drug offense. Our office was already representing his co-defendant. I wasn't really paying too close attention until the teen started raising his voice at Judge Spinoso.

"Sir, I suggest you calm down and lower your voice when you address this court," the judge admonished.

"I'm just trying to tell you that I want another lawyer," the teen responded aggressively. "I don't want the boy wonder here trying to represent me!"

The tension in the almost empty courtroom was suddenly palpable as it bounced off the high ceiling causing the room temperature to soar upward.

"It doesn't work like that," the Judge advised sharply. "I do the assignments here. This isn't the dating game. If you want to hire an attorney of your own, then by all means go right ahead. But since I seriously doubt that you can do that, you need to be grateful that you have a lawyer."

"Grateful my ass!" was the retort.

"Don't you dare use that kind of language in my courtroom!" the judge shouted and almost jumped out of his seat. "Do you understand me? This is not your mama's house! This is a court of law, and I am the judge. I'll throw you under the jail myself if you dare disrespect me again! Do you understand me?"

The judge's eyes were bulging, and his face was flushed and strained. The two uniformed court officers who earlier had been standing in the front far corners of the room, looking bored, now moved closer to the bench as if they were protecting the judge from a sudden ambush by the defendant.

"I don't care what you say?" the kid yelled back. "I ain't afraid of you just cause you got on that robe and got these two old dudes protecting you. All you do is I sit up there and hide behind them. You ain't no man. Talk 'n about throwing me *under the jail*! I just wanna see you try it boy!"

"Sir you are in contempt of court!" Judge Spinoso shouted.

"Get me another damn lawyer!" the defendant roared back and in one swift motion, he turned to John Roberts and spit full force on the side of his face.

The two officers simultaneously lunged at the defendant and tackled him. The podium fell with a large thud as the three men landed next to it on the floor with both officers on top of the defendant. It was only a matter of seconds before they had him completely subdued.

I watched in utter despair as four sheriff deputies rushed into the courtroom, forced the defendant to his feet and escorted him out the side door. John Roberts, who was visibly shaken, was ushered out the same door by Ann Tomlin, the judge's law clerk. Judge Spinoso announced a recess and bolted from the bench.

Because we didn't know how long the recess would be, I didn't think that it was a good idea for me to leave the courtroom or go too far. My cases were next, and both of my clients were young Black men. I didn't want Judge Spinoso to have an excuse to unload on me again for not being there the very second that he decided to come back to the bench.

A few of us lawyers stood in front of the courtroom reflecting on what we had just witnessed. Interestingly, none of us were particularly surprised by any of it. Ours was a tough business- not one for the faint of heart. Outbursts and disruptions, although not an everyday occurrence, came with the territory. It wasn't that long ago that even the idea of something like that happening in a courtroom in this country would have been unthinkable. But times were rapidly changing and the level of overall disrespect for authority was rising.

I tried hard to keep the antics of the people I represented in proper perspective. I had grown to expect foolishness and disrespect from them at almost every turn. None of it had anything to do with me, the only person in the courtroom who I had complete control over. The same was true for the judge too, who apparently needed to learn a thing or two about how to better manage his own responses to negative conduct.

But that didn't mean that none of this stuff got to me. Obviously, it did- more often than I cared to admit. I don't honestly know what I would have done if that kid had spit in my face. It's hard to imagine how dead inside one would have to be to do something so vile to another person. It's doubtful that he would have done that to just anyone. His actions came entirely from an evil place. I felt bad for John Roberts who was just trying to do his job.

Surprisingly, Judge Spinoso wasn't that bad when he returned to the bench. It almost seemed like he had been recharged. He was full of smiles and appeared to be satisfied with himself for some unexplained reason. Perhaps somebody slipped him a Mickey. But it was more than a little creepy. Honestly, I found that to be the strangest part of the entire day.

Regardless, everyone was on high alert for the remainder of the day. I just focused on the task at hand. Fortunately, nothing unusual happened with either one of my cases and both went off without a hitch. I was thankful to God for even small favors.

"I think I would have died right then and there on the spot if someone did that to me," Carla said to me on the phone that night.

I laughed.

"I don't know what you're laughing about," she reacted. "That's the most disgusting thing that I have ever heard."

"I know it's not funny. There's a lot about my job that is *disgusting*. But that's true for a lot of jobs, like cleaning somebody's bathroom or hotel room, or working in a nursing home or in a hospital."

"I guess I don't disagree, but…oh my God!"

"I know."

"That kid is a monster!" she declared.

"And until last week that *monster* was running wild and free up and down the streets of Utica."

"Oh dear!"

"That's why I want you to be more careful," I insisted. "That one day that you and Kiana came to Mama's house by yourself, it wasn't really that safe. I have been meaning to say something to you about it."

"We didn't see anybody," she resisted.

"*That* time. But what about the *next* time?"

"Okay, I hear you," she said. "But I worry about you too."

"Me?" I questioned. "You don't have to worry about me."

"Why not. You're not superman, you know. You bleed just like the rest of us."

"I'm just saying that I lived in Corn Hill my whole life," I contended. "Nobody is going to mess with me."

"That boy in court today doesn't care where you were raised," she argued. "And I bet that there are plenty more out there just like him."

"You're right," I conceded. "But promise me that you'll be careful running around this city trying to find a news story. You're not someone who can easily go unnoticed. I don't have strangers running up to me trying to give me flowers.

"Oh, for heaven's sakes!" she exclaimed and huffed. "You need to let it go."

"And no place is as safe as it seems." I maintained.

"It's really that bad?"

"The same is true for people," I emphasized. "We don't really know who we can trust. Gotta be careful who you let in."

"Okay, I promise," she said. "But you promise me too. You interact with bad guys every day."

"It's a deal," I replied.

"I know I asked you this before but are you going to be in this job forever?" she inquired.

"You don't like my job now?"

"Not particularly," she answered. "I have never liked it."

"Ouch!" I spoke. "What's wrong with it?"

"It makes me nervous."

"How so?"

"You go into the jail to make friends," she explained. "You think it's fun."

"No, I don't," I refuted. "Are you talking about Hasan? Because he's a good guy. You would like him."

"A drug dealer?" she resisted. "I seriously doubt it."

"He's changed," I argued. "And he's in prison, not jail."

"Isn't that worse?"

"Well…yes."

"Why can't you be a regular lawyer?" she pushed.

"What's a '*regular lawyer*?'"

"The guys who wear pinstriped suits and winged tip shoes and who represent businesses and corporations, not guys with guns and three baby mommas."

"I don't know if that stuff interests me," I disclosed. "I think I'd be bored."

"Bored?"

"I don't want to live my life chasing after the almighty dollar," I contended. "The Bible calls pursuing stuff like that '*folly.*'"

"You think you like these guys because they are Black?" she speculated. "Or because they are dangerous, or both?"

"No, that's not it at all."

"Then what is it?"

"It's because they have nothing and no one."

"You can't save the whole world, Sam," Carla expressed. "You are not *Jesus*!"

"I know," I admitted. "But Jesus is my friend."

"Do you even like being a public defender?" she wondered.

"It plays to my strengths so I'm pretty good at it most of the time."

"But that's not what I asked you," she grilled. "You'd be good at a lot of things."

"Maybe."

"What about people like this racist judge you keep telling me about," she continued. "Aren't you tired of dealing with these people?"

"I'm getting there," I admitted.

"So, I don't understand why you aren't at least trying to get out of there."

"Because my life is not my own anymore," I presented. "I don't know if you can understand this, but I made a vow to God that I will do whatever *He* wants me to do. Doesn't really matter to me if I *like* it."

"No, I get that," she asserted. "I think that's great. I really do. But I want you to be happy too."

"I know you do."

"Can't you find a way to please God and enjoy your life at the same time?" she probed. "People do it all the time."

"Do they really?" I challenged.

"My Uncle Sheldon loves being a pastor, and the members of his church adore him," she contended.

"He's burnt out," I blurted out. "He told me so himself that time that I met with him at his church. There're probably not too many jobs more stressful than being the pastor of an inner-city church. People are really messed up."

"Oh, I didn't know that" she responded slowly. "That really breaks my heart. I wish you hadn't told me."

Chapter 18

I was leaving a men's meeting at the church when a young guy, who I didn't really know approached me from behind and told me that Pastor Justin wanted to see me in his office. I immediately turned around and headed back inside. I had no idea what this could be about.

I knocked on the door, which was slightly ajar and opened it halfway. Pastor Justin was sitting alone in his small, sparse office. There was only room for a desk, two chairs and one small filing cabinet. A few family photos were scattered about.

"Hi, Sam. Please come in."

"You wanted to see me?"

"Yes, I did. You can come in. Please have a seat."

I partially closed the door the way he had it and sat down facing him across the desk. He was a good-looking guy with piercing blue eyes and perfectly coiffed hair. He clearly put a lot of thought and effort into his appearance. He reminded me a little of the television preachers, just younger.

He got up and closed the door and returned to his seat.

"Sam, this is a little uncomfortable, but I promised my wife that I would talk to you confidentially."

"Okay," I said and shifted in my seat.

"It's about Kiana," Pastor spoke.

"Kiana?" I reacted. "What about her.?"

"Ah, Marlene recently had a conversation with Kiana, and she is very concerned that Kiana might have … some ideas about you… that you might not be aware of."

"What did she say?"

"I'm really not at liberty to say anything more and again, this is confidential, so I hope that I can trust you not to repeat any of this."

"I'm sorry Pastor but I'm still not sure what this is about?"

"We just think that you should be careful what you say or do with her. Marlene thinks that Kiana is misinterpreting a lot of things about you."

"Kiana knows that I'm not interested in her that way. She's friends with my girlfriend."

"We know that you are with the news reporter."

"Yes, and that's why I can't imagine what she said that I did."

"Sam, please understand that we are not accusing you of anything. She hasn't said anything to lead us to believe that you have been anything but a gentleman."

"Then what?" I questioned.

"We just think that you should be careful around her," Pastor Justin stressed. "Safe to say that her motives when it comes to you aren't entirely pure. She has some ideas in her head… fantasies, shall we say."

"What kind of *fantasies*?" I inquired.

"Let's just say that she is a little fixated on you. We love you both and we don't want to see either one of you to get hurt."

"I have to tell you that this is making me really uncomfortable," I confessed. "It's making me want to distance myself from her altogether. I don't want any hassles from her, and it probably makes sense for me to just stay clear of her."

"I hope that you don't do that," Pastor implored. "Kiana is more fragile than you know. She has a lot of …insecurities. She needs some healing."

"This is unbelievable!"

"I don't disagree," Pastor sympathized. "I know you bring her to church with you on Sundays. I'm asking you to keep doing that until we can figure something else out. She really needs to be around the people of God."

"So, you're saying to pretty much just keep doing the things I'm already doing but to be careful what I say while doing them?"

"Just don't invite her into your life in any way," he advised. "Be intentional about everything with her. Just be a brother in the Lord to her."

"That's all I've ever been!" I snapped before I knew it. I immediately felt bad about my disrespectful tone.

"We know that, Sam," Pastor acknowledged.

"I'm sorry, but um… can I at least tell Carla…er… my girlfriend?"

"I would prefer that you didn't," Pastor Justin beseeched. "We weren't really sure that we should even come to *you* with this, but it seemed the wisest thing to do."

"To be honest, I almost wish that you hadn't told me," I divulged. "Now I feel kinda like my hands are tied a little."

"Right, and I'm really sorry about that," Pastor stated. "This is the first time that we have experienced anything like this in ministry. As a lawyer, I know you understand that conversations between clergy and a congregant are confidential."

"Okay, but should I be watching my back? I mean, is she going to try to set me up or something? Say I tried to rape her? Cause I have seen that."

"I think that you are the last person on this earth who she

would want to hurt."

"Great," I mouthed and slowly exhaled.

"I want you to know that Marlene has committed to regularly meeting and praying with Kiana and trying to help her to stay grounded in reality."

"But what if that doesn't work?" I boldly asked.

Pastor's face suddenly changed from serious to sad. Several wrinkle lines appeared just above his eyebrows and fanned across his forehead. My guess was that he was one of those guys who will age quickly in the face, despite his hard work at trying to prevent and hide the signs of aging. It looked like he started to say something, but then stopped himself. He lowered his eyes.

"Alright, I think I understand," I forced myself to say.

"Thank you, Sam," Pastor said. "I know that we are asking a lot."

I was dejected when I walked out. Obviously, I was aware that Kiana had issues. I also knew that she had some kind of crush on me, which I had dismissed as harmless because I wasn't attracted to her in the least. After all, this wasn't middle school. It's a big world and there are plenty of fish in the sea. I just figured that she would find her way somehow.

But this stuff that Pastor Justin just said was a gamechanger for me in that he inferred that Kiana was struggling badly with her mental health. I didn't want to overreact, but a lot of my clients had undiagnosed mental illnesses, and I knew that this wasn't something that should be taken lightly.

It felt like Kiana was being forced upon me. I really wanted nothing to do with her from this point on, meaning I didn't want to be alone with her or have to engage her in any way. And I wasn't taking her to brunch ever again or going inside her apartment.

The hardest part ended up being not telling Carla what I knew about Kiana. The two were always together and I really didn't want Carla telling Kiana all our business. For some reason, Carla didn't seem to fully grasp that something was seriously off with her friend.

In Carla's defense, however, Kiana was quick-witted and fun to be around most of the time. But she was also devious and underhanded. There was no way of knowing what she would do. The whole thing was unsettling.

In the end, it wasn't really that hard keeping my promise to Pastor. It was only a 20-minute drive from Kiana's apartment to the church. We only ever talked about mundane things, like the weather or church events. About brunch, I just told her that I was working on changing my eating habits, which was true.

• ● •

Four months post-surgery, Mama was doing good. She didn't have any pain, and her doctor said that her scar was continuing to heal nicely. She had resumed all her regular activities. She even walked the three blocks to her church a couple of times in the cold. I had long stopped checking in on her every day and I had to remind myself to call her every week.

But not everything was back to normal. I still hadn't mentioned anything to her about what Tasha had told me about my mother. The truth is that I was very hesitant to bring up the subject because I was afraid of how she would react. We both had grown over time to be slaves to her emotions. That's how she controlled me my whole life.

Indeed, Mama never fought with me the way she did everyone else in the house, especially my mother. But they also all found it easy to ignore her or to yell back at her without restraint.

I couldn't do either one of those things because it bothered me too much to see her upset. As a result, I would do just about anything to keep her happy and placated, even if that required suppressing my honest feelings.

But in all fairness, that was a big part of why I was able to stay on the straight and narrow. I knew that there would be hell to pay if I disappointed or embarrassed her. Most of the guys I grew up with didn't have anybody in their corner like that. And now several of them are buried in graves.

Perhaps part of the lesson here for me was that few things are as simple as they seem, and people are complicated. In response, the Holy Spirit demands that we walk in forgiveness, acceptance, and unconditional love, things that were all very hard for me to do because I had little or no experience with any of them.

However, this newly exposed family secret was like an elephant in the middle of the room to me. Although it no longer haunted my nights, it was all that I could think about whenever I was around Mama. I knew that I needed to hurry up and do something – anything - so that the healing process could start for us. Otherwise, we were forever bound to stay treading in these stagnant waters until we both rotted to death.

Indeed, notwithstanding the fact that she was my only source of support for so long - emotional and otherwise - I felt a strong sense of betrayal. There was no way of getting around that. Everything she did was done intentionally, which meant that she was going to be very defensive. I hadn't a clue how to even begin to have a productive conversation with her about it.

Moreover, I fully understood that there was more to this than my own hurt feelings and personal struggles. Clearly, my mother had suffered a lot more than me. Her life was in absolute shambles, and she was completely lost in this world like most Black people

I knew.

Carla asked me about the situation occasionally. But I was really at the point where I didn't want to talk about it anymore- not even with her. It was just a dead end for me.

Although many of the scars of my past were still visible, they didn't hurt the same way they used to since I became a believer and that was a blessing. However, like Mama with her hysterectomy, I was going to always have some scar tissue. In the end, I prayed about the entire mess and believed for a resolution that would bring healing to our family.

Chapter 19

Apparently, Judge Spinoso told a racist joke in his chambers to a room full of lawyers. It was something about *"why Black people have white on the bottom of their hands and feet."* I wasn't there, so I didn't hear it. Joe from our office was present and he told me. He also told Teresa. He said that nobody really laughed, which I guess is one good thing.

— • ● • —

I went to see Hasan. I didn't have anything new to tell him, but I hadn't seen him in over a month and I felt that I probably needed to touch base with him.

"Because you are already in custody, there is no reason for them to rush," I explained. "Your trial keeps getting moved further down the list."

"I understand," Hasan replied.

"I also think that this is good for you too because I suspect that this other guy is going to struggle more than you with telling a straight story, especially as his memory fades."

"Okay."

"Do you have any more questions for me?" I asked.

"Why are you so serious all the time?" he asked with a chuckle.

"This is serious business," I defended.

"God controls my destiny," Hasan asserted. "I'm not worried. You shouldn't be either."

"I'm working on it," I said.

"Work harder," he responded.

"There are a lot of things that I am dealing with, it's hard to keep the right focus all the time."

"Are you married?' he inquired. "Do you have a family?"

"No, I don't?"

"Why not, if you don't mind me asking."

"No, I don't mind…um…I'm not sure that I am ready to be married."

"Do you got a woman?"

"Yeah, I do."

"Is she a godly woman?"

"Um, she's good, and smart and everything," I presented. "But she's probably not saved, if that's what you mean?"

"It's not your job to save her, you know," he contended.

"I know."

"God loves her just as much as he loves you. He's got this."

"I still worry about her all the time," I said.

"Worry is a sin."

"No, it's not!" I resisted.

"It's the opposite of faith."

"I think it's human nature to worry about the people and things that we care about," I stated.

"That's my point," Hasan argued. "People are born with a sin nature. That's why we all need a savior."

"So, you're telling me that you think it's possible to get to the point where we don't worry about anything?" I asked critically.

"Yes, I do," he replied.

I shook my head.

"What?" he asked.

"I just think that life is hard…"

"You don't have to tell me that," Hasan shot back. "You really think that I don't know that life is *hard*? Look at me!"

"No, I didn't mean it like that, it's just that…"

"We can keep our minds focused on the things we can control," he interrupted. "Worry is our enemy that can be defeated."

"Okay, if you say so," I retreated.

"I get that I probably have less things to worry about than you do being locked up in here and all," he admitted. "But we all have concerns. I just try to focus on the things that I can control, and I can't control what happens with my case. Neither can you."

"I know you're right about that."

"Then what?" he questioned. "You gotta let it go man! All of it!"

"It's just that I always expect the worst to happen because, in my experience, it eventually does, in spite of God," I confessed. "The world is really messed up and so I'm on edge a lot."

"Sounds to me like you don't fully trust that God will see you through," he concluded. Are you blaming him for all that is wrong in the world and in your life?"

"Maybe a little," I admitted. "I don't really know."

"When I was first incarcerated, I didn't know the Lord. I was in a bad place, a dark place that was slowly caving in on me. I was secretly depressed because I was afraid that I was going to die in here…alone. Then that old priest I told you about before told me about a Jesus that I never knew existed and that's when everything started to change for me."

"*Everything*?" I questioned. "You're still in here."

"But that's when the light started to shine in my darkness. Slowly the light has gotten brighter and brighter, and I see things clearer every day."

"I'm happy for you. I really am, but…."

"Don't get me wrong, I want to get out of here in the worst kind of way… I want it so bad that I can taste it," he continued. "This place is not fit for an animal, which is pretty much how they treat us. But if it's God's will that I spend the rest of my life here, I'm okay with that too. I owe him my life."

"Me too," I professed. "I owe him too."

"Then how come your view of the world is worse than mine?" Hasan weighed. "How can that be?"

"I'm not really sure," I muttered.

"Cause from where I sit, you seem to have it all."

"I don't have it all!" I protested. "You don't know. I have people who have been lying to me my whole life. I feel dirty because of it… There's this evil judge lying in wait for me every time I walk into his courtroom… All I do all day is take on other people's problems. Everyday it's somebody different."

I could feel the frustration rising in me as I spoke, but I couldn't hold it back. Now, I was embarrassed that I just told a client all of that. I looked at him and I could see myself reflected in his eyes a little and I suddenly knew how I just sounded.

"Mr. Hicks, excuse me for saying but I think you need to look a little closer."

He smiled warmly and I could only nod my head.

"You still are not seeing things the way they really are," he sympathized.

"Maybe I just need more time," I posed. "I haven't been saved that long."

"Maybe," he conceded. "I read somewhere once that '*a heart that wants to be perfected welcomes the light.*'"

"Yeah… Okay."

"You sure?"

"Yes, I'm sure," I uttered. "Thanks, this helps."

"You're welcome," he said.

I was deep in thought as I left the prison. The cold, fresh wind up against my face and overcoat felt good in comparison to the stale prison air I had been breathing in for the last hour. I got lost in my own thoughts as I drove away. I probably should have been paying better attention. It was the flashing lights from the police car behind me that caused me to immediately regain my focus.

"License, registration and insurance card please," the young, white state trooper requested. He appeared to be barely old enough to drive himself.

I handed him my license and registration card through the driver-side front window.

"I'm sorry," I said. "I think I left my insurance card at home. I just got a new one in the mail."

"Wait here," the trooper ordered, abruptly turned, and walked back to his car, which he parked directly behind me.

He returned after several minutes.

"Get out of the car, Sir!" he directed.

I opened the door and got out of my car. Suddenly, the wind that was somewhat refreshing a few minutes ago was swirling around and felt harsh and abrasive. I followed him to the back of the car and onto the shoulder of the road. Traffic was light with only an occasional vehicle blowing past us.

"Is there something wrong?" I asked.

"It's illegal in this state to drive without insurance," he

reprimanded.

"I have insurance," I refuted. "I told you I left the card at home."

"That means you have no proof of insurance!"

"But didn't you just run my plate," I questioned. "You know I have valid insurance."

"Doesn't matter, Sir," the trooper deflected. "You should not be driving this car on the roads in this state if you don't have proof of insurance."

"What?" I protested. "Are you kidding?"

"Is there a problem, Sir?" he confronted.

He took one step closer to me and we were eye to eye. It was some kind of weird challenge that I didn't quite understand. I hadn't done anything.

"Are you seriously going to write me a ticket for no proof of insurance?" I asked and glared back at him. "Because if that's your intentions, then just do it please."

"I can't let you continue to operate this vehicle if you don't have insurance."

"I'm sorry, but that's insane," I protested.

"How so?"

"Because you know that I have insurance," I argued. "You literally just ran my license plate. You're playing games right now and we both know it."

"What I know is your day is about to get a lot worse if you don't shut your mouth now!" he threatened.

"I already told you, my insurance card is in my briefcase, which I forgot at home. There is nothing else to say."

"Your *briefcase*?" he questioned. "Where do you work?"

"At the courthouse? Why?"

"Are you a lawyer?" he followed.

"Yes, I am. What of it?"

"Do you have a business card?"

"Yes, it's in the car," I barked. "Do you want me to get it? I can read it to you if you want me to."

It was my turn to provoke. He looked me over again with fresh eyes.

"Ah, no… that won't be necessary," he finally said. "Do you know why I stopped you?"

"No, I don't."

He cleared his throat. "You were swerving around in your lane," he alleged.

"No, I wasn't," I resisted.

We just stared at each other for a few seconds.

"I'm going to let you go this time with just a warning," he said in a softer tone than before. "I don't want you to think that I was trying to hassle you. I'm just doing my job."

He immediately turned and walked away.

I got back in my car and sat there for a moment trying to regain my composure. This was the stuff that was so insufferable. Nothing that just happened was for the purposes of keeping the highway safe or for legitimate law enforcement purposes. Rather, it was designed solely to frustrate me and to keep me in my place. We both knew it.

I slowly pulled my car back into the roadway. The police car was still there when I left, and I glanced at it out of my rear-view window as I drove away. I knew that I was very fortunate that this ended the way that it did. From the look in that trooper's eyes, he was looking for a fight.

Indeed, the only reason that I was able to leave that situation when I did, and the way I did – with my sanity intact- was because I had a card in my car that indicated that I was a lawyer. Obviously, not every Black person had one of those. In fact, I was one of just a few Black men the in the entire county who had credentials, which meant that every Black guy who this trooper ever happened to pull over could reasonably expect to be harassed. Although most troopers and police officers admittedly were not like that, it only takes the one.

In hindsight, however, I was wrong too. I let this trooper get under my skin. And it was nothing but my pride that was driving me. The Bible says that *"God resists the proud."* Without a doubt, I could have easily gotten any ticket that this trooper gave me for most traffic violations dismissed in a matter of seconds. I was foolish and acted in a disrespectful manner.

Ultimately, men and women of God today must always walk in integrity. When we don't, we weaken our witness to the world. This means that we ought not be slaves again to our petty emotions, or to our misplaced pride. Our enemy is real and there simply is too much at stake to take the bait. I probably needed to learn that as much as anybody.

Chapter 20

At approximately 11:00 am Monday, a social worker from the county jail called me about Benny Williams, one of my clients. She said that Benny's aunt had just died and that he wanted to go to the funeral on Friday. The problem was that the funeral was downstate in the Bronx and the County Sheriff would not take a jailed inmate to a funeral outside of the county without a transport order signed by a judge. In this case, the assigned judge was Judge Spinoso.

Believe me when I say that the last thing in the world that I wanted to do was to have to ask Judge Spinoso to sign a transport order. Usually, we just walked into chambers and explained to the judges what we needed. It usually took a matter of minutes. But I didn't want to ask this judge to do anything face to face without other people being in the room. In the end, I cowardly gave the application and proposed order to his secretary late Monday afternoon before I went home for the day and just hoped for the best.

I was standing in chambers on Tuesday morning before court was in session with several other lawyers when the Judge turned his attention to me.

"Sam, what's this transport order that you want me to sign?' he asked.

"Benny Williams is in the jail, and he wants to go to his aunt's funeral in the Bronx?"

"I called the jail and it's not his aunt," the judge advised. "It's just some woman that supposedly raised him."

"Oh, she told me that it was his aunt," I responded. "But the sheriff won't transport him without an order."

"But if she's not a blood relative, I'm not sure that the county should pay for that," the judge asserted. "They have to send two officers and it's going to be overnight. That's going to be pretty expensive."

"I know, but he really wants to go, and the sheriff is willing to do it. They just need the order. They do it all the time."

"I don't care what the sheriff is willing to do," the judge resisted. "You lied in your application to me to authorize this trip."

"*Lied* to you?" I reacted. "I did no such thing."

"You said it was his aunt!"

"Because that's what the social worker told me."

"It was your responsibility to get the facts straight before you drafted this proposed order," the judge maintained. "I shouldn't have to tell you how to do your job. I consider what you did to be an attempted fraud upon the court."

"*Fraud*," I repeated. "You must be kidding!"

"Trust me, I'm not kidding at all," the judge said. "I take things like this very seriously."

"It doesn't matter whether or not he's a blood relative," I argued. "There's nothing in the transportation policy that requires that they be related."

"It matters to me."

"Why?" I asked.

"I already told you… and I don't have to answer to you."

"Because you don't have an answer," I boldly asserted. "You

probably didn't even read the policy."

"Once again, Mr. Hicks, I suggest you watch how you speak to me," the judge warned. "I will have none of your insubordination."

"I'm sorry Judge, but please imagine how you would feel if you were in my client's shoes."

"He should have thought about that before he broke the law."

"I don't think that's fair," I replied. "He's awaiting trial. He hasn't been found guilty of anything."

"Unfortunately for you, I'm the one they pay to decide what is *fair* around here," the judge mocked. "I'm not sure that you really want to try to take me on."

"What?" I asked. "*Take you on?*"

"I've already made a few phone calls," he said. "Just you wait and see!"

"Careful Judge, the white part of my hand knows how to dial the phone too," I said before I knew it.

"What's that supposed to mean?" he demanded.

"I think you know."

"I have half a mind to report you to the bar association," Judge Spinoso threatened.

"When you do, please make sure that you tell them I said that you are the most racist judge that I have ever appeared in front of," I goaded.

"Now, here it is," the judge ridiculed. "Everything with you people is about race."

"Nope," I replied. "Nice try, but everything with '*you people*' is about race!"

"I think you need to leave my chambers!" he stated loudly.

"I can't believe that anyone can be so cold-hearted," I provoked. "You're supposed to be the face of justice!"

"Don't you dare presume to tell me how to do my job."

"So, what now?" I asked. "You're telling me that you're not going to sign the transport order?"

"I haven't decided that yet?" he snapped.

"Well, the funeral is Friday," I declared. "That's in three days. The sheriff needs to know as soon as possible for staffing purposes."

"Yes, you did say that in your papers, but it's hard to know what to believe with you."

"When will you decide?" I questioned further.

"I can't tell you that either," the judge insisted. "Now please leave my sight!"

I threw my hands up in the air in disgust and looked around the room for some support. Most everyone just quickly put their heads down. I slowly turned and marched out of the room.

Teresa wanted to know everything that I said to the judge. I recounted the exchange as best as I remembered. The more I recalled, the angrier she got … at me.

Her face was beet red when I finished. But I didn't care. In my mind, this was inevitable. The judge was, in fact, looking for excuses to come at me, especially when others were around. I had requested that she do something about the situation time and time again and she chose to ignore me. This was all her fault.

To be clear, I wasn't sorry for anything that I said to this judge. Although I was angry and didn't say everything perfectly, I wasn't out of control. This didn't happen in open court. We were off the record in chambers. I was fighting hard for my client, which was something that I had taken an oath to do. Everyone in that room would have done the same thing, or later wished that they had because they would have lost the respect of some of our peers.

Moreover, this was different than my prior encounter with the state trooper on the side of the road. This was business, my business! I'm pretty sure that if Benny Williams was there that he wouldn't have thought that I overreacted or was unprofessional. Even poor people were entitled to good lawyers who fight hard. Unlike my encounter with the trooper, Judge Spinoso didn't have a gun under his robe that he could have pulled out and shot me dead right then and there- at least as far as I knew.

Sadly, Teresa seemed to be mostly concerned that the judge was going to take my *"lack of judgment"* out on the entire public defender's office and that this was going to somehow impact upon her personally. I really didn't understand either concern. However, she clearly wasn't concerned at all about Judge Spinoso' s deliberate attempt to assassinate my character, or that he might try to get me sanctioned or disbarred.

But I didn't argue with her. Instead, I quietly listened as she vented. I felt like a child being reprimanded by his mother for not eating his broccoli. I was disillusioned. I was tired too.

The judge's secretary called our office early Thursday morning. She said that Judge Spinoso signed the transport order, and someone could come pick it up. When I called the social worker to let her know, she said it was too late to schedule the trip.

Thereafter, the judge and I mostly ignored each other, rarely making eye contact. I heard that Teresa apologized to him on my behalf for my behavior that day. She never told me that she did that. However, she did banish me from going into chambers for any reason and said that someone else from our office had to cover for me when it was necessary that I be there. That was a win for me as far as I was concerned. I truly despised this judge.

Unfortunately, my relationship with Teresa deteriorated greatly after the incident. She was distant. Apparently, I went from being her shining star to her problem child in about two years. I was holding resentment too, which I knew was wrong. I felt like she didn't have my back and that I could only depend on God himself in this battle against evil.

Chapter 21

Carla called me and said that she wanted to go to a concert for Valentine's Day. The idea sounded great to me at first until she told me that she wanted Kiana to come with us.

"I don't get it," I protested. "Why does Kiana have to come?"

"Because she really wants to go. Besides, it was kinda her idea."

"She really wants to go to a concert called, '*An Evening for Lovers*?'" I questioned.

"Yeah, why not?"

"Because she ain't got nobody to call baby," I callously answered.

"Sam!"

I laughed.

"She really likes one of the performers," Carla pleaded.

"Then you guys just go," I said. "I don't want to go with her."

"But I want you to go too, *Tiger*. It's Valentine's Day!'"

"Don't call me that."

"You usually like it when I call you *Tiger*."

"Not when you are trying to use your womanly charms against me. I'll have you know that I'm a strong Black man and I'm not falling for your little bag of tricks!"

"I thought you liked my *tricks*."

"Not this one," I said and laughed hearty, which probably was a mistake because I'm pretty sure she knew right then that she had me.

"C'mon, Sam," she zeroed in. "It'll be fun. What else do you have planned for Valentines Day? You probably haven't even thought about it."

"The concert is the day before," I replied. "We can just do something by ourselves on the actual day."

"But you'll like it," she insisted. "It's gonna be nice. It's three different singers. You can pretend that it's just the two of us."

"I already told you that Kiana is starting to get on my nerves."

"I don't know why. She respects you a lot."

"She's too much," I contended.

"You don't even have to talk to her" she insisted.

"I don't know…"

"Okay, it's decided," she interjected. "I promise you won't regret it."

"Is that right?"

"You know you can trust me, *Tiger*!"

"You know, you're not gonna get your way all the time," I tried to say.

"I know because, '*you're the man and what you say goes*.'"

"I hate it when you patronize me," I whined.

"I don't even know what you're talking about," she feigned.

— • ● • —

The concert was at the Turning Stone Resort Casino in Verona, New York, approximately 26 miles west of Utica. It was new, and I had never been there before. Turns out it was a great venue. It was mostly a Black crowd, and the event was sold out.

One of the singers was from Brooklyn and that's apparently how Kiana knew about her. We had good seats and Carla sat in the middle.

The music was phenomenal. There were no original songs. The performers covered mostly slow jams, and it seemed like the entire crowd sang along out loud as people swayed to the music. I sneaked a peak at my beautiful girlfriend every chance that I got. She looked like a dream in a tight-fitting red dress and held on tight to my right bicep, which she squeezed every so often.

At one point, the host invited couples who were in love to stand to our feet and engage in an exercise where we turned and faced one another, held hands, looked deep into each other's eyes and repeated the following after him:

There is no place in the world--
Where I would rather be tonight--
Then standing here with you--
And looking into your beautiful eyes--
And professing my eternal love and gratitude--
For all the world to see--.
You have captured my heart and my imagination—
While soothing all the pain away--
And elevated my very existence—
High above the moon and the stars--
I give you my whole heart—
To have and to hold--
For you have settled my soul--
Sweet lover of mine--
Happy Valentine's Day--

I could barely get the words out at the end as I was so caught up. The showroom erupted in applause as we kissed and held each other tight for a few precious, stolen seconds. Anyone could see that we were in love. This woman was so under my skin that it scared me and shook me to my core. I didn't know- or care- what the other couples were doing… or Kiana, for that matter. For me, it was just about me and my girl.

Overall, it was a magical night. I truly enjoyed myself and I was able to relax and forget about my many issues. Carla was right and I was glad that she dragged me out of my bad mood.

Kiana was quiet during the ride home, but she didn't seem detached or withdrawn in any way that I noticed. It was almost midnight when we left the casino. Nobody really said much of anything. The air was crisp but the temperature outside wasn't too bad. A blanket of newly fallen snow covered the roads.

Carla was fast asleep as I pulled into Kiana's apartment complex to drop her off. She said a quick goodbye and ran fast to her door. My hope was that she got the message and that any *fantasies* that she still harbored in her head about me were put to rest for good.

———— • ● • ————

Christina was pregnant again. This time she was far enough gone to let the whole family in on their carefully guarded secret. Once again, Carla was thrilled beyond words, as was the entire family.

"Do you want to have kids one day?" I asked.

"Me?"

"Yeah."

"I have dreamed about being a mother my whole life. Most girls dream about their weddings. I dreamed about loving my children."

"Really?"

"Yes, it's true."

"You never said anything before," I said.

"You never asked."

"You're right, I didn't."

"I have a lot of surprises up my sleeves," she joked.

"So how many children do you want?"

"Oh, I don't know," she hesitated. "Probably like two or three. It depends on the sex because I want at least one boy and one girl."

"It's hard raising kids today," I replied. "I think that I would be worried all the time that something was going to happen to them."

"There you go again seeing only the dark side."

"Huh, it's interesting that you put it that way," I remarked. "Someone else recently said pretty much the same thing to me."

"It's true," she dug in. "I always told you that you are way too negative."

"When you have been in the dark so long, it damages your eyes," I contended. "It's hard to see clear, but my will is getting stronger. It's a constant fight."

"My therapist taught me that some things simply can't be diminished," she said. "I'm supposed to try to focus on those things. For me, I can't imagine that anything could be better than holding my baby close to my heart. I can hardly wait. The rest of it doesn't matter."

"Even your career?"

"Motherhood would be first for me," she revealed. "Then being a good wife. I want a career too, but it's secondary. My mom was mostly focused on the three of us, more than on selling houses."

"I think that you're going to be a wonderful mother," I said.

"You do?"

"And auntie," I added.

"Thank you."

"You're welcome."

•●•

Mama rarely came out of her house this time of year. Having been born and raised in Mississippi, she claimed to have never really adjusted to the New York winters. She always blasted the heat in her house so that it felt like Mississippi in the summer. I always hated that she did that because it made everything inside so dry.

"Hey, how you been," she asked as I walked in through the doorway. She was sitting in the living room watching television.

"I'm good. How are you feeling?'

"I told you I'm fine," she replied. "I want everybody to stop asking me that."

"Where are you on your meds?" I questioned. "Do you need refills?"

"I still got enough of my pills," she reported. "I'm tired of taking them too."

"But you *are* taking them?"

"Yes, why wouldn't I be taking them?"

"You know how you get sometimes."

"How's that?" she asked.

"Stubborn and hard-headed."

"You want a cup of coffee?" she asked. "I just made a pot."

"No, I'm trying to cut down… What have you been up to

lately? I know you probably haven't left the house since I was here last week."

"I sure haven't," she indicated. "I'm not going out in all that mess and catching the death of pneumonia."

"There's no such thing!" I maintained.

"Say what? I don't know what you're talking about."

"So, what have you been doing?" I inquired.

"Katrina stopped by to see me."

"Who?"

"Katrina! You know, Carla's friend. She came over that one time when I got out of the hospital."

"You mean *Kiana*?"

"Yeah, that's the one," she said. "You know I can't remember all these crazy names."

"Kiana came here?" I pressed.

"She was just checking in to see how I was doing. She brought flowers. There they are there."

She pointed to the vase of purple and white flowers on one of the end tables.

"By herself?" I questioned. "Carla wasn't with her?"

"No, Carla didn't come."

"I wonder what made her do that?" I asked myself aloud.

"I thought the same thing," she commented. "You ain't messing around with her? Are you, Sam?"

"What?"

"You heard me," she insisted. "You ain't messing with that girl too?"

"Absolutely not!"

"Well, something in the milk ain't clean," she suggested. "I smell something fishy."

"I don't know what you smell, but it's not my doing," I

asserted.

"Cause I know I raised you better than that," she stressed. "Ain't nothing worse than a two-timing man!"

"When was she here?"

"The day before yesterday."

"What did she say?"

"Nothing much that I recall… She just talked nice, you know. That's what put me to mind that she was up to something." "How did she get here?" I wondered.

"She had a car."

"Really? I didn't think she ever drove her car."

"It was a little white car with a big dent on one side. You know, one of those real little ones. She parked it out front and I watched her get in it from my window when she left."

"That's so odd," I said. "You okay?"

"Child please, that girl ain't studying me. I suspect she's fixed on catching herself somebody else's man."

She stared me down.

"Not a chance," I dismissed. "Never gonna happen."

"Carla know her girlfriend is a snake in the grass?"

"No, I don't think so."

"You better tell her before that hot thang tries to bring you down with her," she advised. "Women are always a step or two ahead of men."

"I don't think that's true," I said.

"Trust me, I know what I'm talking about."

"That's because none of the men you have been with have been anything to brag about."

"I know that's right," she admitted. "That's how come I know."

"So, *you* made bad choices," I argued. "That's on *you*.

Nobody else."

"That's what I'm trying to tell you, all of the choices were bad," she maintained. "Things were different back then."

"Not that different," I resisted. "There is nothing new under the sun."

"I can't speak for nobody else, but I did the best that I could," she submitted.

"Maybe the right thing to do was to trust God and just go it alone with just him," I presented. "Sometimes it's better that way. God never intended for us to settle by making a deal with the devil."

"It's hard to be alone your whole life," she argued. "You don't know how much it…."

"Is letting some demon use you and then leave you crushed and broken into a thousand little pieces better?"

She didn't respond.

"Was that little bit of pleasure really worth all the pain?" I criticized.

"That's easy for you to say," she pushed back. "You got Carla. She loves you."

"No, it's not," I resisted. "My own father was king of the snakes. He used you and he used my mother who was just a kid."

"Who told you that?" she snapped. "You don't know everything about how it went down!"

"Doesn't matter, it's true," I calmly stated. "We both know it's true."

Her eyes got big, and she began slowly rubbing her hands together. She looked troubled.

"None of that was my fault!" she protested. "I told her to stop running around the house half-dressed and…"

"It wasn't Janet's fault either," I defended. "You get that, right? Grown men shouldn't be having sex with girls, no matter how you think *it went down*. It's a crime. He should have gone to prison. *You* should have made sure he went to prison. What happened ruined her life."

"Maybe it did," Mama acknowledged and turned away from me. "Don't you think I feel bad about that?"

"Then maybe you should forgive her for whatever you think she did to make this happen."

"When did you talk to her?"

"I haven't spoken to her at all," I refuted. "She doesn't want to talk to me! You know she hates me. My guess is that she blames me too for how her life has turned out. That's why she never loved me."

"That's why I loved you for her," Mama appealed. "I never let her do anything bad to you…ever!"

"I know," I replied. "But it still wasn't enough. I still almost lost everything."

"What do you want me to do?" she questioned. "This is all water under the bridge. What's the sense in bringing all this up again now?"

"It's a mistake to just keep sweeping our dirt under the rug. It just makes things worse for us as a family. Everybody sees it."

"Sometimes that's all you can do," she contended.

"If you love me, then help my mother find some peace," I urged. "No one should have to live their whole life feeling that bad about herself."

"I don't know how to do that," she muttered. "That's not on me."

"Mama, can you please at least try…for me."

She just stared at me with a blank look on her face that slowly started to twitch.

"Please just think about it," I begged.

She was quiet… fighting. It's hard to fight a demon who has for years fortified a stronghold within. I knew this firsthand.

"Mama?"

She maintained her stoic expression. Then she blinked her eyes and nodded her head ever so slightly in quiet assent.

———— • ◉ • ————

I told Carla about my conversation with Mama the first chance I got. She said that she was proud of me because of the way that I handled it. I was proud of the way Mama handled everything. I expected her to be a lot more indignant.

I had rehearsed that conversation maybe a thousand times in my head like it was the closing argument in the biggest trial of my life. I thought it was important that I not let Mama get me angry and that I keep her on point. Nobody ever won any argument in our family or acknowledged any fault or mistake - ever.

I also reported Kiana's unannounced visit to Mama's house to my girlfriend. She thought it was odd, but not too troubling.

"I wouldn't make a big deal out of it," she said. "Kiana probably was just trying to be thoughtful."

I didn't tell Carla what Mama thought Kiana really was trying to do. Or that I was more than a little spooked by the whole thing because this was starting to feel a lot like Kiana was stalking me.

Chapter 22

There was a hit-and-run accident in the city of Utica involving a drunk driver on Burrstone Road near Utica College. Tragically, a young woman was walking along the side of the roadway just after midnight on a rainy night when she was struck by an oncoming car and thrown into a small ditch. Her body was found the next day by an early morning jogger.

The incident was heavily covered by the local media. The victim was just 19 years old. Two days later, a white college student turned himself into the authorities. It was prearranged by his parent's lawyers who accompanied him to the police station. The arraignment was scheduled for the next morning.

Bail was denied the young man in city court, which meant that he had to stay in jail. His lawyers made a bail application the next day in county court before Judge Spinoso. The district attorney's office vehemently opposed the granting of any bail claiming that they feared that the defendant would flee the jurisdiction in that his only tie to Utica was the college. Notwithstanding, Judge Spinoso set bail at $250,000 cash or bond. Thereafter, bond was immediately posted, and the defendant was released from custody the same afternoon.

Apparently, something happened between Judge Spinosa and Frank Lloyd, the district attorney, related the bail. I only heard about it secondhand through the rumor mill in the courthouse, but it was all that everyone was talking about. People were saying that the two men had gone toe to toe in chambers about the granting of bail with threats and obscenities being tossed around like small missiles. They had to be separated.

At the risk of sounding petty, I was glad that somebody else besides me was mixing it up with this judge. I felt like I was vindicated a little even though what happened had nothing to do with me or my office. The undeniable truth is that more times than not, the county court judges went along with the bail recommendations coming from the district attorney's office, regardless of how outrageous they were. This was an anomaly.

———•●•———

I ran into Judge Spinoso on the elevator in the courthouse. I immediately felt trapped. He was the last person with whom I wanted to be riding alone with in an elevator. It was awkward for both of us, and we initially just nodded our heads and looked away.

"Sam, I know that you think that I harbor some ill will towards you, but I can assure you that I do not," the judge spoke into the deafening silence. "I want you to know that I'm actually rooting for you."

"Thank you," I whispered without making eye contact.

"I think that it's wonderful what you have accomplished in your life," he continued. "It's couldn't have been easy for you. I know you just got a job to do, and you probably don't like these people you have to represent any more than the rest of us do."

I responded only with a forced half-smile and maintained my defensive posture of focusing all my being on the small hole in the corner of the carpet. I secretly cursed the elevator for being so slow.

"There was a Black student that I knew at Holy Cross," the judge offered. "One of the brightest guys I ever met. And he worked hard too. He earned his own way; I can tell you that. He didn't wait around for somebody to give him a handout."

"Really?"

"His name was Perry something…no Andrew Perry, that's it. Great guy. I lost track of what happened to him. You don't happen to know him?"

"Ah, no I don't."

"So, I know that there are good Black people just like there are good white people," he pointed out. "I never judge people by their color. I just wanted you to know that."

"Thank you for telling me," I replied just as the elevator door mercifully opened and I got out as fast as I could. I was starting to perspire heavily, and I could tell that my heart rate was elevated as I fought with all the different thoughts and emotions rushing through me in rapid succession.

<hr />

I received a phone call at my desk from a lawyer. He said his name was Tony DiLauro. I didn't recognize the name. My initial thought was that he was from the bar association, and he was investigating a complaint against me from Judge Spinoso. It had been a while since the judge had made that threat and I hadn't heard anything. But Mr. DiLauro said that he wanted to talk to me about a business proposition.

We met at one of the small Italian restaurants downtown the next day for drinks. In fact, this was the same restaurant where I met Carla for the first time. A part of me was still concerned that this was some kind of trap. I told myself that I needed to be careful what I said to this guy.

I arrived on time and Mr. DiLauro was already seated at a table. The restaurant was nearly empty as it was 2:00 pm and the lunch crowd had pretty much emptied out. He was a middle-aged white man with a full head of dark hair and a closely trimmed beard. I smelled his cologne as we shook hands. It was a clean smell that I kind of liked.

"Sam, it's nice to meet you," he began. "Thank you for giving me this time. I know that you must be busy."

"It's not a problem," I replied. "It's nice to meet you too."

"Can I get you something to drink?"

"No, I'm good."

"Let me get right to it then," he said.

"Okay."

"I'm a partner at McMann & Tatum. I don't know if you have heard of us. We are a small firm that does mostly civil work. We represent a lot of banks, and we do a lot of real estate. There is only me and Tom Burton. We have one associate, Jake Russo, who likes finance and business."

"I see."

"We are thinking about expanding into some other areas."

"Like what?" I asked.

"We want a trial attorney. Most of the matters that come into the office that requires real litigation we end up referring out. Tom and I have no experience with that kind of stuff."

"When you say litigation, are you talking about plaintiff's work or defense work?"

"We're not really sure. We would mostly leave that up to the person we hire."

"Okay."

"I guess the purpose of this meeting is to gage whether you have any interest in working with us. I have heard a lot of good things about you. I followed closely that big kidnapping case you had a couple of years back."

"That case was almost the death of me," I admitted. "It probably aged me ten years."

"Everyone in the courthouse have nothing but good things to say about you. I hope you know that."

"I don't know about that, Mr. DiLauro," I replied somewhat sheepishly. "I think that you probably just didn't talk to the right people."

"Call me Tony."

"Okay."

"I heard that you are tough and smart," he advised. "You're a fighter and that's what we want."

"But I have only been out of law school for 4 years," I said in earnest. "And I don't know much about civil practice. I have only ever done criminal defense."

"I get that," he replied and shrugged his shoulders. "That's why we would be willing to let you build your own practice. Obviously, we want to make money, but you can pretty much learn as you grow with us."

"I must admit that it sounds interesting," I replied. "I just never…"

"You have to be tired by now of all that crap in the public defender's office," he interrupted. "I interned with legal aid in New York City when I was in law school, and I know what a rat race it is. It can eat away at your soul if you let it."

"Hmm, I don't know what to say?" I admitted.

"Just say that you'll think about it," he quicky interjected. "I know that it would be a big change for you. We do a lot of work with not-for-profits, like churches and charities, and this would be an opportunity for you to still help the same people who you are currently representing."

"I am interested, but I really have to think about it," I said.

"Certainly, I understand," he answered. "If you are ever ready to make the switch, then give me a call."

He handed me his business card.

"Thank you," I said. "Thank you very much."

"If you want to know more about us, I can set up something so that you can meet Tom and Jake, and we can see whether we can somehow make it work."

"I appreciate that," I replied. "I can't thank you enough for thinking of me. I know that this is a great opportunity."

"It's been my pleasure," he asserted. "You are an outstanding young man. I really admire what you do."

"Thank you."

I had no idea what kind of law I wanted to practice when I graduated from law school. I would have taken just about any job that wasn't in New York City. But I had learned so much about myself since graduation. I enjoyed the trial work, and I was improving at it every day. It was just the other stuff that was weighing me down. Truthfully, I never really saw myself working long hours in a law firm trying to make enough money for them to earn my keep.

For some reason, I was hesitant to mention my meeting with Mr. DiLauro to Carla. I was concerned that she would pressure me to leave the public defender's office because of the way she felt about my job. But I really didn't like keeping things from her.

"Are you really thinking about it, or did you just say that to be polite?" she questioned over dinner.

"Probably, a little of both."

"Sounds to me like they really like you."

"I'm afraid that it might be too slow for me," I explained.

"It also sounds like you won't be representing these Black kids with guns anymore. Is that it for you?"

"No, I hate those cases. They are all the same, but I do know how to handle them."

"I know you're good at it," she stated.

"Honestly, I don't want to waste whatever talent I have on trying to win some money for some little old lady who fell in the parking lot at the bingo hall."

"I'm sure that that would mean the world to that old lady," she contended.

"Maybe so, but I just don't think that would be enough for me."

"Well, I think you really should just think about it," she set forth. "The ball is really in your court. You already have a job, so it's not like you have to just take this offer?"

"That's true."

"And my guess is that you are more marketable than you think," she presented. "Maybe, the point is for you to be open to doing something different. I'm guessing that the rest will just work itself out for you."

"Yes…that makes sense to me. Thanks."

"You're   welcome."
How'd you get so smart?" I came back.

"It's a gift," she replied with a chuckle.

"You have a lot of gifts," I said in a flirtatious tone.

"Why thank you, Sir."

———•●•———

It was another cold grey day in Central New York. A horn sounded just as I was being escorted across the yard by a corrections officer at Marcy Correctional Facility to the SHU to meet with Hasan. Almost immediately, a host of men exited the buildings and came outside. They were walking toward us. It's hard to say how many there were exactly, maybe two hundred or so. Apparently, they were headed to lunch.

It was almost like an out of body experience for me. As the men approached, they were careful not to get too close to us. Like the parting of the Red Sea, I just saw a wall of green uniforms dividing before me. I tried hard not to gawk, but it was hard not to stare because I was very much captivated by the faces I saw. They were both young and old, short and tall, healthy and tired looking. They were also mostly Black, or men of color.

Obviously, I knew that a large percentage of the men confined there were minority. But to see it on full display in living color like that was shocking and feelings of dread and sadness overcame me. It felt like someone close to me had just died and I immediately started to grieve before I came to myself and suppressed all of it. I was there on business.

"I'm sorry that I can't get out here more often to see you," I expressed sincerely.

"I understand," Hasan replied. "I know that you are busy."

"Like I said before, there is no real rush to do anything with this case because you are already confined."

"Yeah,   you   said   that."
"But the ADA just made us a new offer yesterday."

"Anything good?"

"No, not really. They want 3 ½ years minimum. I think we should reject this

offer too. It's probably not their final one and we can still go to trial if they never offer us something acceptable."

"Okay, makes sense," Hasan said.

"So, what else?" I asked. "What's going on with you?"

"Nothing really."

"Are they ever going to put you back in general population?" I wondered.

"They gave me a year in here."

"A year in solitary confinement! Are you kidding?"

"No, I'm not kidding," he answered matter-of-factly. "But it's probably safer for me like this. It's no fun having to watch my back all the time."

"But a year?" I questioned. "I didn't even know that they could do that. Sounds cruel. Aren't you going stir crazy?"

"Maybe a little, but I have my books and my Bibles. And exercise, I get that too."

"Is that enough?"

"It is for now," he claimed. "I'm in prison."

His words landed with a loud thud in my head. "I have no idea how you do it."

"I'm alive!"

"Yes, you are alive, but how do you wake up every morning and face the new day knowing that it's probably going to be just more of the same," I pondered.

"I'm also the son of the Most High."

"Right?"

"So, I still have joy," he asserted.

"But how do you find any joy here?" I questioned. "Seems impossible to me."

"Because I'm still fully connected to God who is the source of my strength."

"But you are also a man in the prime of life who is essentially caged up all day," I articulated.

"More than being a man, or even a Black man, I have been grafted into the family of God," he presented. "I'm a Christian. That's my true identity now."

"We are *new creatures in Christ Jesus*," I recounted.

"Built to last!" he emphasized.

"You have this way of looking at things that is so simple," I commented. "It makes me feel petty and ungrateful in comparison."

"I think that you are way too hard on yourself," Hasan observed. "We shouldn't let anyone make us think less of ourselves."

"I know I am."

"You got to get out of your own head, man," Hasan scolded. "*Jesus said that he didn't come into the world to condemn man.*"

"*He came to give us an abundant life*," I finished with the Bible reference.

"It's a waste of time beating ourselves up over things we can't change. Maybe you should use that same energy to build up your faith."

"I know, but..."

"*But* either God is God, or he isn't," he argued. "Either you trust him, or you don't, to give your life real meaning."

"I hear you, but I just don't think that it's that easy," I resisted

"Sure, it is."

"When I look around, all I see are hurting people, including Christians." I insisted.

"And there is nothing good in your life?" he postured. "Nothing at all?"

"I didn't say that?" I defended.

"Mr. Hicks, you should try focusing on the good things. We

talked about this before."

"I know."

"I mean just look around you now," he prompted. "I don't know how these guys who don't know Jesus come out of a place like this still in their right mind."

"I have to say I don't know either," I reflected. "It's kind of amazing."

"But I will do it because *the greater one lives in me*."

"Right."

"He lives in you too."

"I know he does."

"So, nothing else really matters," he asserted. "The other things are just flesh wounds."

"*Flesh wounds*," I repeated to myself. "I like that."

"You know, I don't think that God can really use people who don't trust him all the way," he spoke

"Really?" I reacted. "Why not?"

"Because you can't live off of somebody else's testimony for too long."

"Oh… that makes sense," I admitted.

"That means that we all have to take it to the gut sometimes," Hasan explained. "I can take the pain of living. So can you. It becomes part of *your* testimony."

"Okay…but do you ever cry about the injustice and pain?" I entreated.

"Me …*cry*?"

Hasan opened his eyes wide. Clearly, the question caught him off guard and he wasn't comfortable with it.

"Yes, just asking," I pressed.

"I actually cried a little the other night," he disclosed under his breath. "It was nothing really. I was good by the morning."

Chapter 23

Both pastors liked to greet as many of the congregation after Sunday service as they could. It was very informal, and people tended to stand around the front of the sanctuary waiting for an opportunity to approach one of them. I personally never did that. I just figured that they were probably tired after ministering all morning and I didn't want to be the one keeping them from their rest.

One Sunday, Kiana had a short meeting with the worship people right after service. I was standing in the back of the sanctuary waiting to drive her home when I noticed that Pastor Justin was standing up front alone. Our eyes met and he smiled warmly and waived to me. I decided on the fly to go up and talk to him.

"Hi, Sam."

"Hi Pastor, how are you?"

"I'm good."

"I don't want to take up too much of your time, but I was wondering how it was going with Kiana?"

"Kiana?" he questioned.

"Yeah, I have been trying to do what you suggested and keep boundaries with

her. But last week she showed up uninvited at my

grandmother's house."

"Really?"

"Yeah, it really wasn't that big of a deal," I was careful to say. "My grandmother is still recovering from the surgery she had a few months back and Kiana just showed up and brought her flowers."

"I see."

"And if she can drive herself there, then she can drive herself to church on Sundays," I asserted.

"Was there a problem at your grandmother's house?"

"Like I said, it wasn't a big deal. But she doesn't really know my grandmother. They only met once. My grandmother thought it was odd and cautioned me."

I could see Pastor Justin struggling to find the right words. He began slowly, "So, I can say that Marlene has met with Kiana a few times. I think they talked a couple of times over the phone too. I don't know everything. The bottom line is that Kiana really wants a relationship, and she is very frustrated that she hasn't met anyone. There's more to it, but that's it in a nutshell."

"But I'm involved with her friend," I maintained.

"Sadly, a lot of the women in the church share the same struggle," he explained. "They want a good *Christian* husband, but there aren't a lot of single men to be found. The whole thing can be very depressing."

"I get that," I admitted.

"It's just easier that way for men," he continued. "All we can really do is encourage people to trust God and try to be patient. It's a cross to bear. Especially, for women who want to have a family."

"When it comes to trusting God, I struggle with that myself," I conceded.

"Then you get what I'm talking about," Pastor stated. "Believe me, I didn't understand why my mother got cancer and died when I was 19 years old. I didn't want to hear anything about God at that time even though I knew then that I was called to the ministry."

"So, what did you do?"

"I treaded water for over a year while I grieved the most devastating loss any boy could possibly know," he revealed. "I almost didn't make it. I almost drowned. I'm not proud of it, but I eventually came around."

"I'm sorry but I don't follow," I begged. "How did you *come around*?"

"The comforter, who is the Holy Spirit, came and gently pulled me back to shore."

"And just like that you started believing in him again?" I questioned.

"What's the alternative? To live a depressing, debilitating life, where I am angry with God and angry at the world?"

"There probably isn't anything else," I admitted.

"Exactly," he echoed.

Pastor looked lost in that moment, and I immediately felt bad for my part in making him drift back down to the dark water. But he only languished for a few seconds before coming back to the surface and being fully present again.

"It's important that we don't let what we don't know rob us of what we do," he declared. "And one thing we know with absolute certainty is that God is good to his core."

"Right."

"Sam, God understands our frustration, he really does," he added. "But we still have to do it his way because our way is never better."

"Okay…okay," I replied and let the idea settle within me. "Thank you, Pastor."

"I will tell Pastor Marlene about Kiana's little excursion to your grandmother's house. And again, we very much appreciate your patience with this matter."

As I was walking away from Pastor Justin, I decided that I needed to work on changing my attitude about Kiana. Although I grew up in a house full of females, I always knew that I could be a little tone deaf myself when it came to many of the unique issues that women faced. It was just that they were always so loud and mean-spirited with each other that I just stopped listening to them most of the time.

Similarly, I was focused primarily on how much the situation with Kiana annoyed me that I never once took her very real feelings into consideration - the same way that I never truly considered my mother's pain either. Rather, I just wished that they would vanish completely from my life.

But I was having a change of heart. The Bible says that *mercy triumphs over judgement*. That meant that I didn't really want to be in a position where I was judging either one of them. That was just too much weight for me to carry.

The drive from the church to Kiana's apartment was awkward. She was quiet for some reason. Usually, she did most of the talking while I focused on the road. I was so determined to keep her at arm's length and to not give her anything that she could misinterpret, that I possibly was a little rude. I felt bad.

"My grandmother told me that you stopped by her place the other day?"

"Yes, she's so sweet."

"*Sweet*?"

Kiana laughed.

"Yeah, I like how tough she is," she explained. "She tells it like it is."

"Not always."

"You know what I mean, Sam. She has probably seen a lot in her life. It makes you hard?"

"Do you think that's a good thing?" I asked.

"What do you mean?" she pressed.

"I think my grandmother never learned how to deal with her pain and disappointment in a healthy way. She has pushed people away- hurt them."

"She probably had to do that."

"Why do you say that?" I solicited.

"Cause our pain is different."

"Whose pain?"

"You can't understand," she asserted.

"Try me," I replied.

"It's still a man's world you know."

"I don't dispute that," I conceded. "But we all got pain."

"Like people in my family have said that about me too," she disclosed. "They think that I'm always pushing them away. But I do that because I don't trust them with my real feelings. So, I only show them so much."

"That sounds incredibly lonely," I commented. "And sad, like you're hiding your real self."

"Maybe it is, but most Black girls have to do it for ourselves."

"I get that, but everybody feels like that from time to time." I deflected. "You have to trust somebody too, right?"

"Why do I have to trust anyone when I already know what is going to happen?"

"Healthy relationships require trust," I preached.

"*Healthy relationships*?" she sneered. "I don't even know

what that is."

"We have to trust God," I defended.

"To be honest, sometimes it's hard to trust even him because from what I have seen you can pray and pray for something until you're blue in the face and he still doesn't answer."

"You don't mean that."

"Yes, I do!"

I glanced over at her to see her looking straight ahead with a kind of glazed look on her face.

"You ever think that maybe the answer is *no*." I asserted. "Or just no for now?"

She jerked her entire body and threw me a scathing look like a poison dart. Her searing eyes got big as they filled with pain and resentment.

Seeing her torment up close, I retreated slightly using a softer tone, "Sometimes we just have to pray for something else altogether different, even if it's just the strength to wait on him to reveal his perfect will."

"You sound like Marlene," she said soberly as she shifted her body sidewise away from me and stared out the passenger side window. "It's different for white people too."

"I'm sorry. We're only trying to help."

"Don't you have a scripture you want to quote at me too?" she condescended.

I didn't know how to respond... or what to think. It was my turn to look away.

"Like I told her too," Kiana expressed from her heart. "I feel like I've been waiting my whole life for something that's never gonna happen. And I'm sick and tired of all this Christian mumbo jumbo."

"I'm sorry Kiana. I really am sorry."

"My '*momentary affliction*' is killing me!" she declared in a manner that caused the temperature in the car to instantly chill.

"Everybody has to wait for something," I spoke before I knew it and couldn't stop myself. "It's called life."

"Oh, okay," she muttered and rolled her eyes. "I'll just fast and pray about it a little more. That should do the trick."

She looked totally deflated.

Chapter 24

Teresa's edict that I stay out of the Judge Spinoso' s chambers lasted only two weeks. I had too many cases with him for that to be workable. Particularly, I needed to do my own negotiations with the prosecutors, and they kept asking for me. Also, it was important to me that the Judge not think that I was avoiding him or, worse yet, that I was afraid of him.

Apparently, the feud between the judge and the district attorney was still ongoing. The case with the college student who killed the young girl was still regularly covered in the newspaper and I noticed the added tensions whenever the subject of bail reduction came up for anyone. This judge seemed determined to make it clear to them that his word was law and that he didn't care what the district attorney's office thought about it.

We were in Judge Spinoso' s chambers when John Wildman, the ADA, told me that the guy who Hasan was charged with stabbing had attacked another inmate with a homemade knife at Sing Sing Correctional Facility, in Ossining, New York. As a result, the prosecution was willing to reduce Hasan's charge to a misdemeanor assault charge with no additional jail time.

"Let me get this straight, you are going to reduce a felony charge where a guy was stabbed in the heart and almost died to a simple misdemeanor?" Judge Spinoso questioned.

"Yes, we talked about it, and we think that this is the right thing to do under the circumstances," John defended.

"I don't agree," the judge resisted.

"We can't continue to prosecute a claim that we can't prove at trial," John admitted.

"You can still prove it," the judge argued. "Just do your job. You guys put this case into the grand jury, not me."

"With all due respect judge, the second this victim stabbed another inmate, it shows that he has violent tendencies of his own that severely weakens our ability to present him as a victim. How can we believe anything he says?"

"Just use other witnesses to corroborate what you already told the grand jury happened," the judge reflected. "It's hardly rocket science."

"That's the thing, this happened in a state prison," John explained. "There are no other witnesses who are willing to testify. Nobody saw anything."

"Well, I'm not comfortable going along with this big of a reduction," the judge declared. "I have an ethical obligation to uphold the law."

"We do too," John replied.

"Then we all want the same thing … except for Sam here, who just wants to get his bad guy with *violent tendencies* of his own back out on the streets again as soon as possible," Judge Spinoso said and turned to look directly into my eyes.

I felt myself tighten up inside. I glanced over at John, who quickly put his head down.

"Isn't that right, Sam?" Judge Spinoso baited.

"Excuse me judge, but we all took the same oath," I finally spoke.

"Really? he reacted. "That's news to me. So, you wear the

robe too huh?"

I didn't respond, which was hard for me not to do because I had a response burning a hole on the tip of my tongue. But I was afraid of what Teresa would do if I got into another go around with this judge. I didn't want to lose my job.

Clearly, someone needed to be the bigger man. I was beginning to understand that I needed to learn a little more restraint as words are powerful and true followers of Christ ought to be slow to speak. We are called to be light in the world, which I found to be easier said than done.

Moreover, I was starting to see this thing the way that Hasan did. Specifically, this really wasn't my battle to fight. Hasan said that he was trusting the Lord in all of this. That meant that his trust wasn't in me or my advocacy skills as a lawyer, and it would have been a mistake for me to make any of this about me.

Ultimately, this was all good for Hasan. Now that I knew that the district attorney's office had no real interest in prosecuting this case, there was no way that I would ever allow Hasan to plea to anything other than a misdemeanor. Besides, we had a very good chance of winning the whole thing if we decided to take this case to trial.

Just as I was walking out of chambers into the courtroom, I heard someone call my name faintly. I turned back and saw the familiar face of a Black woman who appeared to be in her early 30s. My initial thought was that she was a former client, or the relative of someone who I had represented in the past. I was trying not to stare.

"Hi, Sam."

"Hi," I replied as I quickly tried to figure out who this person was.

Her dark complexion was dull and lifeless. She looked hard

and malnourished, like someone with an active addiction. Her hair was cut short like a man, and she wore a man's bomber jacket that was highly worn and too big for her. She also smelled like cigarette smoke.

"It's me, Kamika," she said as she stood to her feet. "Remember me? I used to be with Janet for a minute."

"Yes, of course I remember you, Kamika," I responded half-heartedly. "You were at my grandmother's birthday party a few years back. How are you?"

"I'm hanging in there," she said and walked with me into the hall. "I'm here waiting for them to call my girl's case. Her name is Natisha Jones. Do you know her?"

"No, I don't."

"They got her out at the jail on some bogus assault charge. She didn't do nothing.

I keep trying to tell them. Lasandra hit Tish first. I saw the whole thing go down. That chick deserved what she got, know what I mean?"

"Yes," I obliged. "I'm sorry."

"I don't see how they can just take one person's word over somebody else's."

"I know they do that," I affirmed.

"Is there something that you can maybe do to help her?" Kamika asked.

"I'm not her lawyer."

"How's Janet?" she quickly pivoted.

"I wouldn't know," I said. "I haven't seen her in a while."

"Me either. I miss her though, man. She's good people."

"Yes, she is," I forced myself to say.

"You probably don't really think that on account of how messed up she is, but she got a good heart, you know," Kamika expressed. "It's just that she gotta act like she's so big and bad all the time. I tried to tell her that she should just chill a little, but she don't listen to nobody."

"No, she doesn't." I agreed.

"I tell you, yo mama is all the way live."

"Yes, she is."

"She talks about you all the time though."

"*Me*?" I recoiled.

"Yeah, you! She's proud of *you* bro!"

"*Proud*?"

"Yeah, whenever she gets her drink on, she gets real and that's when she starts talking about you being a lawyer and being so smart and everything. That's how I know what I'm talkin about."

"Really?" I questioned. "Because I have a hard time believing that."

"Cause you don't know her," Kiana asserted. "She thinks you hate her, and that you think you are better than her."

"*Better than her*?"

"She knows you blame her for not being a good mother. She cries a lot about it whenever she's getting lit."

"Are you kidding?" I asked. "She brought a lot of this on herself."

"Y'all still family you know," she pointed out. The nicotine smell was intense, and I had to turn away for a second.

"I know that."

"She wanted to be a good mother to you and the twins, but she didn't know how."

"She never even tried," I contended. "I'm sorry, but she wasn't there most of the time. She disappeared sometimes for weeks at a time."

"Nobody was ever there for her either!" Kamika shot back. "That's the reason she's mean as a ole ally cat."

"What's her thing now?" I asked pointedly. "Is it alcohol, or does she do other things too?"

"I ain't never seen her wild out too much. She likes her Hennessy though… when she can get her hands on it. Buy her that and she's straight."

"Is there something else that I can do for her?"

She winced. "Like what?"

"I don't know," I replied. "I guess I just want to know how I can best help her?"

"You want to *help* her?"

"Yes, I do." I stared at her. I was shaking slightly within.

"Since when?" she challenged.

"Since now."

"Um…she just wants you to *like* her."

"*Like her*?"

"Yeah, you know, act like you respect her just cause she's yo moms."

"*Respect her*?" I repeated.

"There's a difference between mama and grandmama, you know."

"Yes, I know."

"You probably have never even asked her anything about herself like you are trying to ask me now," she argued.

"I have never been able to talk to her about anything," I answered defensively. "Nobody can talk to her."

"That was when you were a boy," Kamika asserted. "But you supposed to be a man now. So, man up!"

It felt like she punched me in my chest as hard as she could. But I didn't react outwardly because I didn't want Kamika to see the impact that her words had on me. The sudden pain, however, traveled like an electric current directly into my heart and forever changed its rhythm… I inhaled big and then allowed my lungs to deflate slowly.

"…Okay …I got it," I whispered.

"You gotta crack the nut to get to the meat, you know," Kiana argued.

"Right."

— • ● • —

Carla's take was that my mother was drowning in guilt, which to me was contrary to the way that someone who truly felt bad about something that they had done typically acted.

"I disagree," Carla explained. "This is a woman who doesn't have a relationship with any of her three children, not to mention her mother or grandchildren. You don't think she has regrets?"

"That's the way she always wanted it."

"No. it's not."

"Yes, it is," I resisted. "She never bought us anything. Not on Christmas or on our birthdays. Not even a telephone call to wish us a good day. That's the kinda stuff Black men do who typically only care about spreading their seed around."

"You don't understand trauma," she asserted. "She has a severe, lasting sense of shock and hurt. Everything she does probably gets filtered through layers of emotional and psychological pain. It must be maddening!"

"So, I don't know trauma?"

"Sam, you can't really expect the things she says and does to make sense. That's all I'm saying."

"Okay, but she's hurting other people too, people who don't

deserve to have her pain thrown in their faces every time they try to talk to her."

"She's sick," Carla expressed. "Try thinking of it like that. What if she had cancer?"

"What if she did?" I contested.

"Would you blame her for being a little cranky?"

"*A little cranky*?" I repeated. "That's like saying that a rabid dog is a little *wild*."

"Sam, you know what I mean."

"Okay, maybe she is *sick* like you say," I conceded. "I'm willing to do whatever I can to help her. I really am."

"Then what is it?" Carla asked in earnest.

"I just don't want to be blamed for her being the way she is for the rest of *my* life. I didn't have a say in how I came into this world. She's not the only one who feels guilty."

"You don't know that she blames you."

"Yes, I do," I protested. "A part of me wishes that she would have just aborted me."

"Oh Sam! You don't mean that!"

"It all started with what my father did," I contended. "She's probably been telling herself for years how much better her life would have been if that never happened, and she never got pregnant."

"Her friend told you that she was proud of you," Carla pointed out.

"Yeah, well, she's got a funny way of showing it."

"Are you saying that you wish that you were never born at all?"

"Um… no, I'm not really saying that" I replied. "Although I really do think that there are worse things than never having been born, such as being born severely disabled or something. The truth is that I wouldn't want to have missed out on loving you… and having you in my life."

"Oh my… I don't know what to say," she whispered. "You have a way of catching me completely off guard every time."

"I don't do it on purpose."

"I know…that's really the thing."

Chapter 25

Unexpectedly, a man from the New York State Commission on Judicial Conduct came to see me at the office. I was in court at the time in the middle of a motion argument, and I couldn't come right away. He ended up waiting for me for nearly an hour in our conference room.

"Sorry to keep you waiting," I said as I rushed in. "What can I do for you?"

"My name is Jim Price," he began. "I am here investigating a complaint we received against Judge Spinoso."

He was a white man in his 50s. He was short and thin with a receding hair line and thick, round glasses. The black suit he was wearing was wrinkled a little and I thought he looked like one of those guys who stood at the front door of a funeral home during calling hours.

I was suddenly very anxious.

"What kind of complaint?"

"I really can't tell you that?" he said.

"Who filed it?" I asked.

"I can't tell you that either."

"How can I help you?" I inquired.

"I was hoping I could ask you a couple of questions?"

"Sure, go ahead."

He opened a worn brown briefcase and took out a yellow legal pad and a gold pen. He put the pad on the table in front of him.

He was very deliberate in his movement, and I had my defenses up and fully engaged.

"You appear in front of Judge Spinoso on a regular basis, isn't that correct?

"Yes, I do."

"How often would you say?"

"Several times a week. I have most of my cases with him."

"Have you ever felt unfairly treated by him?"

"Me personally?" I sought clarification.

"Yes."

"Ah… yes I have." I stated.

"How so?" Mr. Price pressed.

"Um, I don't think that the judge likes me very much."

"What makes you say that?"

"He has said several things that gave me that impression," I said. "Ever since he came on the bench, he has gone out of his way to embarrass me in front of other attorneys."

"Do you think that he treats you differently because you are Black?"

"Yes."

"Do you remember telling him that he was 'the most racist judge that you ever appeared in front of?'" Mr. Price questioned from his notes.

"Yes, I said that."

"Did you mean it?"

"Yes, I meant it."

"Have you ever heard Judge Spinoso make any racist jokes or comments?"

"He has referred to our clients as monkeys and circus animals. He hasn't really made any jokes in my presence, but I know for a fact that he made jokes when I wasn't there- everybody knows."

"I see," Mr. Price muttered to himself as he wrote on his legal pad.

"He told me on the elevator one day that he doesn't like any of my clients. He is routinely condescending to me in an abrasive way and treats me differently than he treats everyone else."

"And you think that is because you are Black?"

"Yes, I do."

"No other reason?"

"No, I do my job."

"How would you respond if I told you that the judge says that you are often disrespectful and unprepared?"

"Sounds like him," I simply stated.

"If that is true, then why haven't we heard from you?"

"Me?" I questioned.

"Yes."

"You mean file a complaint against a judge who has threatened to come after me personally?" I asked critically.

"How did he threaten you?"

"Um, for one, Judge Spinoso threatened to report me to the bar association. He said that he had already made some calls. He demanded that I leave his chambers once in front of other attorneys and..."

"Excuse me, did he say who he called?"

"No, he didn't."

"I'm sorry, I interrupted you," Mr. Price said. "Please go ahead."

"I told my boss several times that this judge was out to get me," I continued. "She ended up reprimanding me and ordered me to stay out of chambers. After that, I didn't think that it made much sense for me to make a big deal out of the way he was treating me. I didn't feel like anyone would back me up so that it would be my word against his. I'm the only Black attorney in this county."

"Yes, I know," Mr. Price acknowledged. "And that's the thing. I think that gives you more power over this situation than you know. We would have listened to you."

"I had no way of knowing that" I insisted. "He's the one in the black robe."

"But you were aware that you have an obligation to zealously represent your clients, many of whom are Black and minority. You are also an officer of the court."

"So are a lot of other people who stood around and witnessed all of this and did nothing," I argued. "Are you suggesting that my obligation to the bar was somehow greater than everybody else's because I'm Black?"

"No, I'm not suggesting that at all."

"Then what?" I asked.

"It happened to *you*," he stressed.

"I know it happened to me."

"Please, I'm not criticizing you, just trying to understand," Mr. Price explained. "If you really thought that this judge was so racist, didn't you want to at least try to bring your observations to our attention in an attempt to protect your clients from him?"

"I guess that I didn't trust that you would do anything about this injustice," I boldly spoke. "He probably wasn't qualified to be a judge in the first place. Like I already said, there is only me here. If I get fired, then there will be none."

"That's a lot of pressure on your young shoulders," he observed.

"It's not more than I can bare. I've been through worse."

"I see," Mr. Price said and looked down at his notes while he regrouped.

We were both tense. I could hear the heat blowing overhead from the vent in the ceiling.

"Is there anything else that you can tell me that you think we ought to know about Judge Spinoso's fitness for the bench?"

"No," I answered definitively.

"What would you like to see us do about him?"

"I don't know," I said. "It's not my call."

"Do you think he should be removed?"

"I can't really answer that," I punted. "I guess that depends on if he sees that he has a problem and wants to change. I doubt that is the case. He came to us like this and probably will never change on his own. But nobody who is the way he is now should be standing in judgement over people who are already broken and spend most of their days struggling in the margins."

"Well said," Mr. Price complimented.

Still uneasy, I just looked straight ahead. I wasn't enjoying any of this.

"Okay, then I think that is all I need for now," Mr. Price said as he stood to his feet. "I know that I don't have to tell you that this conversation is completely confidential."

"Yes."

"You can call me at any time if you think of anything else," he offered.

He handed me his business card.

"Okay, I will."

"And Mr. Hicks," he said, "I just want you to know how sorry I am about all of this. I can't imagine how hard this has been on you. My sister is married to a Black man who happens to be a lawyer too in Cleveland. He is a great guy and a wonderful husband and father. He has told me some things that he has seen and experienced, but nothing quite like this. It really bothers me that you feel so… um… alone in this... I just wanted to say that."

"Thank you," I replied as he reached out his hand. I was surprised by his strong handshake.

I escorted him out, and he thanked me again, turned and walked out the door. I felt empty inside. I headed to my small office, closed the door and sat there for about an hour in the dark… thinking alone.

I was interrupted by a knock at the door. It was Teresa. She opened the door and turned on the lights.

"Who was the man who came to see you earlier?" she asked. "They told me that he was from the state?"

"He was from the State Commission on Judicial Conduct."

"What did he want?"

"He had some questions about Judge Spinoso."

"Did you call him?"

"No, I didn't."

"Did you file a complaint with them or something?"

"No."

"Then how did he know to talk to you?" she insisted.

"I don't know. He didn't say, but he obviously had spoken to someone."

"Well, I don't like it," she said. "This could jeopardize everything that we are trying to do here."

"*Jeopardize* how?"

"If word gets out that you are speaking to the people who investigate judges, he might come after us."

"What's he gonna do, Teresa?" I posed. "The man is evil. He can't possibly be any more unfair to us."

"Oh yes he can!" she disputed. "Just you wait and see."

She looked frazzled. I felt sorry for her. I took a moment to let the churning in my stomach subside.

"I don't have to wait," I asserted.

"What do you mean?"

"I am resigning my position here," I spoke slowly. "I just decided."

I could hardly believe my own mouth. I felt the blood rush to my head and my entire body tensed up.

"*Resigning*?" she repeated.

"I will be leaving in 30 days."

"Can I ask where you are going?"

"To one of the law firms here in town," I revealed. "They made me an offer that I can't turn down."

"Is this because of Vito Spinoso?"

"Partly."

"What else?"

"Why do you want to know?"

"Because I do, and I think you owe me an answer," she maintained.

I hesitated again. "Let me ask you this, why didn't you file a complaint against him on behalf of all of the Black people we represent?"

"I don't know what you mean." she lied. Her voice was suddenly shaky.

"I think you do," I maintained.

"Sam, I don't like this," she resisted. "I feel like you are accusing me of something, and I don't appreciate it."

"I'm not accusing you of anything, Teresa. But whoever filed this complaint apparently thought I was being routinely mistreated and that our clients weren't getting a fair break. What do you think?"

"I know that you have been going through a pretty tough stretch. I'm sorry about that, but …"

"*A tough stretch*?" I raised up. "Are you kidding?"

"Yeah, we all have them," she defended. "Do you think that it's easy doing my job? You have no idea how easy it is for me to get jammed up with all that is happening around here all the time. The county can cut our budget at any time. I am barely holding it together as it is!"

"No, I wouldn't want your job," I acknowledged. "But unfortunately, I don't want mine anymore either."

She looked wounded. Her eyes were intense and brooding as she crossed her arms in front of her and sulked.

"Are you sure about this, Sam?" she asked softly.

"No, I most certainly am *not sure*."

"Then why don't you take some more time to think about it?" she suggested.

"Because I don't need any more time. I'm just tired."

"It's really that bad?" she questioned.

"Yes, it is."

Her face dropped.

"I'm sorry, I didn't fully realize," she whispered.

"I know you didn't."

"So, 30 days, huh?" she repeated.

"Yes, you will have my resignation letter on your desk tomorrow morning," I advised. "I don't want to leave you short-handed, so just let me know if you need more time to find someone to replace me."

Chapter 26

"What do you mean you've never been to Niagara Falls?" Carla said and winced.

"I never really ever thought about going there," I replied.

"What? It's only like 200 miles from here."
"I know."

"I love it there," she expressed. "I used to go there like three or four times a year when I was a kid. Some of my best memories growing up are of walking around the state park there with my family."

"What's the big deal?" I questioned. "It's just a big hole with water and mist in it."

She looked at me in disgust. "I feel like I don't know you at all. Seriously, who are you?"

"I'm just trying to understand."

"See, now we have to go," she insisted. "You don't know what you're missing."

"I guess we can go sometime." I jumped up from her sofa and started cleaning up the mess that I had made on her coffee table.

"No, gotta go this weekend," she pressed.

"I can't go this weekend."

"Why not?" she asked. "It's spring break."

"I don't want to go there now," I resisted. "It's still cold outside. I have asthma."

"No, you don't. You're just being a big baby!"

"Maybe later on in the summer."

"I want to go for a long weekend," she pleaded. "This may be the last time we get to do something before you start your new job and get all caught up. You know how you are."

"But you're talking about going in like four days."

"I'll make the arrangements," she offered. "You don't have to do anything. Oh my God! I know the perfect place!"

"Well, I don't know," I hesitated. "You know I don't like to get my hair wet."

She rolled her eyes. "Don't worry, it's not one of those big chain hotels. It's small and quaint. Ooh…I'm getting so excited already. I don't know why I never thought of this before."

"Isn't it too late to get reservations?" I asked.

"It's off season and my mom knows the man who owns the place."

"I'm blaming you if I get sick," I whined.

"You won't get sick," she maintained. "You're gonna love it. I promise!"

I was just giving her a hard time. I always wanted to see the falls but just never got around to going there. I knew that she had her free-spirited side and needed to regularly roam the earth. It had been a long winter. I had no problem tagging along, although I preferred warm weather excursions.

————— •●• —————

After giving it considerable thought, and praying about it, I decided to double down on keeping clear boundaries with Kiana.

I really did feel sorry for her because some people probably die from heartache and loneliness. But she continued to make me feel uncomfortable the way she acted like I was her *church boyfriend* all the time. Hopefully, she can start driving herself to church.

I also felt a little like Carla and I were flaunting our relationship in front of her. I get that we often acted a little giddy when we were together. That had to hurt- a painful reminder that she was all alone. But it wasn't fair for her to expect us to hide our affection for each other. I didn't think we even knew how to do that.

However, I was still convinced that it was a mistake to bring Kiana with us to the casino on Valentine's Day, even though we ended up having a great time. But she also chose to come with us when she could have just as easily stayed home. So, that was on her.

My sense was that Kiana had been through far worse than this and she was a survivor. Carla told me that Kiana talked a lot about how she was raised in poverty. She was an only child and was often left alone. Apparently, her parents never married and fought frequently. She was bitter about all of it.

Sadly, as Pastor Justin pointed out, the predicament that she now found herself in wasn't unique to her. There were single woman everywhere dealing with the same issues. The truth isn't always easy to hear- or to live with.

Sometimes we all have to honker down and wait out the storm. Before Carla, I was literally dying a slow death my whole life. Then one night, there she was on my television doing the local news. The point is that everything can change in a moment.

Carla took Kiana home with her to Webster for her sister's birthday luncheon with a group of girlfriends. According to Carla, Kiana fit right in and was the life of the party. There was a lot of baby talk and, presumably, a good amount of male bashing. My dysfunctional family aside, it was my impression that women, generally, did a good job taking care of their own. No doubt, Kiana was in good hands that day.

Oddly, Mama asked me about Kiana.

"What's going on with that gal that stopped by here to see me the other day?"

"Who? Kiana?"

"Yes, that's the one," Mama said. "Did you ever find out what that was really about?'

"No, not really."

"Did you tell Carla that her girlfriend is all up in her business?"

"I told her that Kiana brought you flowers, if that's what you mean?"

"What did Carla do?"

"What's she supposed to do?" I recoiled.

"If it was me, I would put my foot on her head like the Bible says."

"The Bible doesn't say that!"

"Yes, it does," she refuted. "It says that Jesus put his foot on the devil's head. My mama used to talk about that all the time."

"But that's not what it means," I maintained.

"I'm trying to tell you that heffa is up to no good."

"Maybe, but I already told you that I'm not involved with Kiana in any kind of way."

"She goes to church with you, don't she?"

"Yeah."

"And she rides in your car?"

"Yes, but…"

"And people see ya'll together, just the two of you siting close together?"

"Yeah, all that is true, but…"

"She might not say anything, but she's wanting to get with you," Mama concluded. "In her heart, that's what she wants. I know about women and you being a good-looking man too. Lord have mercy!"

She shook her head from side to side several times and looked at me critically evincing her disbelief and disappointment about how naïve she thought I was being.

"You really think so?" I asked.

Mama glared at me. "She's gonna try you just as sure as I'm standing here. looking you in your face."

Chapter 27

It was lightly raining when we arrived in Niagara Falls on Friday night. I was very worried that the entire weekend was going to be a wash. The air temperature was 56 degrees, which I could handle. But rain was going to ruin everything for me.

The accommodations was a little one-bedroom cottage in the heart of Niagara Falls, just 2.2 miles from the American Falls. It had a full kitchen and a small patio. We brought groceries with us and cooked all our meals. It wasn't secluded exactly, but there wasn't a lot of people around, especially at night. The sound of silence was very seducing. It was easy to imagine that we were miles from civilization, like Adam and Eve in paradise.

We walked to the falls and spent one afternoon at a museum and window shopping. We even did a little hiking, which turned out to be not too bad. I started to overheat at one point. Although the humidity was high, it never rained hard. She ended up braiding her hair in two rows that made her look like a teenager.

We mostly just held hands and talked and laughed like we did when we were in Jamaica. She told me stories that I never heard before about her youth and her family vacationing together in the area. She seemed different -like a beautiful rose just before full bloom. This was clearly her fix, and I made a mental note to always remember that she needed adventure from time to time.

At night, we read to each other, ate chocolate chip cookies she had prepared and listened to music on my boom box, which she told me to bring. One night we slow danced on the patio in the dark and I got high off her. The wind had a pretty good bite to it, and I held her as close to me as I could. I could feel my love burning like an infernal and I prayed to myself and asked God to never let this time together end because I knew down deep in my soul that nothing could ever best the moment- nothing at all.

The last night was hard because neither one of us wanted to leave this perfect place. I never felt closer to anyone. Somehow, I had managed to push everything else out of my mind except how much I loved her. I didn't want to have to go back to obsessing over other people's problems.

"So, did you have a nice time?" she asked as we lay in bed.

"The best!"

"Really? You really did?"

"Yes, can't you tell?" I reacted.

"I thought so, but I didn't want to ask."

"Why?"

"Because I was having the best time too and I didn't want to ruin it by asking too many questions."

"Nothing means more to me than being with you," I declared. "More than anything, I need for you to believe that even when we can't be together. I believe that God created us for each other. You're His greatest gift to me."

"I love it when you say things like that," she whispered. "It brings healing to my soul."

"I love you, Carla."

"I love you too, Sam."

We fell asleep like that. I didn't dream about anything that night because I was holding my dream in my arms. It was the sweetest sleep of my life.

The next morning, I started packing the car, while she cleaned up. We made a good team. It was a clear, sunny day and we were ready to leave early.

"I have an idea, why don't we drive back down by the falls where you showed me before for one last look? "I asked. "Who knows when we will be back here again? I want to get a picture together there."

"Okay, if you want to." she said. "I just have to check the bathroom one more time to make sure that I didn't leave anything."

"Alright, I need to take the trash around back and I will be waiting in the car."

"Okay."

She looked happy as we drove away. I rubbed the top of her thigh, and she smiled at me. It was already starting to get crowded even though it was just 8:00 am and it took me a few minutes to find a parking spot. There were several people in the vicinity, including people with small children who were running around in circles.

"Hey buddy," I said to a young man standing there in a small group. "Would you mind taking a picture of me and my girlfriend?"

"No, not at all," he replied with a big smile.

"We want to go over there so that we have the falls in the background."

"Okay, no problem," he said.

The three of us walked the short distance together in silence."

"Carla, where do you think?" I asked.

"Um, let's see…over there," she pointed.

We walked over to the place she pointed to, and I gave the

guy my camera. We posed close together, smiling big. He was a nice guy. He took several shots as she directed him.

"Oh, I have an idea," I said.

"What," she asked.

I immediately dropped down to one knee and took her hand before she knew it.

"What are you doing?" she asked. She looked confused.

I nervously mumbled the words that I had been secretly rehearsing in my head all weekend:

I always knew you were out there somewhere, but I honestly never thought I'd find you. I prayed for you even when I didn't know how

to pray, or who to pray to. I'm not ashamed to say that I cried for you

too every night in my secret place in the corner of my heart, and I

longed for you... It was hard to breath before you... I was basically

numb with no chance of ever truly living... And then one day, you suddenly appeared out of nowhere … and in a moment, my crazy, messed-up world was realigned, and everything

started to make sense. Truthfully, Jesus saved my soul, but you rescued my heart. I literally don't think that I can live another minute without you, not another second. Please don't let me die this way. Carla, I'm asking you to be my wife. Will you marry me?"

"Wait a minute," she said. "We never talked about getting married."

"I know we haven't."

"But what if I'm still not, you know… healed inside?"

"I don't care. We can go the rest of the way united together as one body."

"You want to marry me?"

"Yes, I'm ready to love you with my whole life."

"Really, you do?" she asked again and opened her eyes wide.

"I have this to prove it."

I fumbled around in my pocket for several seconds and finally took the small box. out of my pocket and opened it and handed it to her. She took it and started sobbing.

"Carla, you okay?"

She just stood there shaking. I rose to my feet and took her in my arms. She cried hard as we clung to each other. I cried too, a little.

"You okay Carla?" I whispered. "I didn't mean to upset you like this."

"You didn't *upset* me you jerk!" She pushed me gently.

"Then what? Do you like the ring?"

She came to herself and looked at it again.

"Wait…wait a minute!" she hesitated and deeply inhaled and breathed out in a rush. "Is this my grandmother's ring?"

"The diamond is," I said. "I had it put in a different setting."

"You did?"

"Obviously, Christina helped again," I readily disclosed.

"But where did you get it?" she asked.

"From your mother."

"My mother just gave this to you. But she said…"

"She said you always wanted it and that she's been saving it for you," I explained. "Is it okay? I can get something else if you want."

I could see the wheels turning in her head. Then she erupted in tears again and put her head down. But this time it was more like a mixture of tears and laughter. Her face was a complete watery mess. It was the first time that I ever saw her not look that good.

"Carla?" I whispered. "People are watching."

"…Carla?"

"Will you marry me?... Will you?"

She nodded her head before pressing it into my chest.

She cried off and on for the next hour or so. I wasn't expecting that. Most of the time, she had her emotions on lockdown like a teenager on detention for breaking curfew. I couldn't fully grasp why this came as such a surprise to her. People were asking me about it all the time.

"I have another surprise," I said in the car.

"What is it?"

"We are stopping at your parent's house. We are due there at 11 o'clock so we have to hurry."

"I was just thinking about us maybe stopping to see if they were home," she stated.

"Christina is going to be there too."

"Hmm…don't think that I don't know that all of this was a conspiracy headed by my mom," she stated. "You know, it was her idea that we come to Niagara Falls in the first place?"

"No, you didn't tell me that."

"Yeah, she kept talking about how it would be a good break for me. She's been pushing for us to be together since the first time she met you."

"That's because she doesn't know that I used to be a drug dealer and a pimp. Better not ever tell her."

"Stop it!" she reprimanded. "Why do you have to ruin everything?"

I just laughed and said, "I don't understand why she likes me so much."

"I think she likes that you're grounded," Carla explained. "She doesn't like guys who are extroverts. She thinks that they can't be trusted."

"That doesn't seem fair," I indicated.

"She has her reasons for feeling that way," she admitted. "I probably gave her … reasons."

"I think that she's just impressed with my manliness," I joked.

"Christina thinks she likes that you are Black and professional. She wasn't exactly thrilled at first when Christina started dating Eric. They are cool now, but it took some time for her to warm up to him."

"I'll take whatever I can get," I said. "I like your mother, but I don't want to get on her bad side."

"She never said anything to me about the ring," Carla disclosed. "I never thought she would ever give it to either one of us. She had to fight to get it from my aunts."

"When Christiana is her name Christina or Christiana and I were getting your Christmas present, your mother mentioned the ring."

"How did she '*mention*' it exactly?"

"She just said that she had something for you and for me to call her before I proposed to you."

"Oh my God!" she reacted. "That's so embarrassing!"

"No, please don't be," I begged. "I felt supported, not pressured. It's the stone you wanted right?"

"Yes, it is. It's perfect!" She stared down at her ring again.

"I don't know the first thing about engagement rings and getting something on my own would have really stressed me out," I admitted. "I just wanted to get you something that you would really like."

"I loved my grandmother," she offered. "She would let me

play in her jewelry box all the time- something that my mother would never let us do."

"I'm sure that your grandmother would be happy to know that you have it."

"Yeah, probably," she said. "I can hardly believe it!"

Considering everything, we were relatively quiet for much of the drive. I was having a hard time focusing and my thoughts were all over the place. I think my brain completely short circuited at one point. I missed our exit on the New York State thruway because I forgot where we were going. I felt stupid.

As we pulled into her parent's driveway, there were about ten cars parked there. We just looked at each other in disbelief. Then we started laughing. And suddenly we couldn't suppress our glee any longer. We just sat there deliriously happy and holding on to each other. We didn't care if anyone saw us. We were soaring together … both of us so grateful to be alive!

"Come on in here, Sam," Carla finally said. "Looks like we gonna jump the broom before sundown!"

————— • ● • —————

The headline in the Utica Observer-Dispatch read *State Judicial Group calls for removal of Utica Judge*. Specifically, the article reported that the State Commission on Judicial Conduct urged the Court of Appeals to end Justice Vito Spinoso's tenure on the bench after it investigated complaints of racial discrimination. The judge was found to have regularly engaged in racially offensive, profane remarks about Black people. Apparently, several assistant district attorneys reported instances of misconduct, including an incident on the golf course where Judge Spinoso purportedly told a racially charged joke. It was also reported that the judge, who denied the allegations, had been suspended with pay pending an appeal to the Court of Appeals.

The courthouse was all abuzz with the news. Surprisingly, I had a mixed reaction. I was very happy that Judge Spinoso was being called-out. But I was also embarrassed that I never filed a complaint with the commission myself. I should have elevated the matter. Mr. Price was correct that I had dropped the ball completely. My distrust of everyone in the system across the board had gotten the best of me.

Moreover, although I didn't doubt that everything that the guys in the district attorney's office reported that they had seen and heard Judge Spinoso do were true, for them this was about their feud with him over bail release- nothing more and nothing less. In this regard, I had grossly misjudged the depths of their anger concerning the matter. Notwithstanding, it was clear to me that they never would have filed the complaint in the first instance had they not been on the ousts with the judge, regardless of how many offensive jokes he told. That's why I should have been the one to do it.

Nobody asked me about Judge Spinoso or whether I had filed a complaint, although I'm certain that many people assumed that I had since I was the only Black attorney who regularly appeared before this judge, and I was resigning my job. I was careful not to publicly express any opinion about the matter.

Interestingly, I didn't hear anyone criticizing the district attorney's office for bringing this abuse of power to light. In fact, they were being portrayed as heroes even though they had admittedly betrayed their golf buddy, who had mistakenly trusted them enough to be his authentic self around them. A few people said that they felt bad for the judge, but they really didn't elaborate further.

Chapter 28

I drove to Kiana's house to pick her up for church like I had been doing for over a year. I pulled up in the parking lot in front of her apartment building and waited for her to come out. She was a no-show. I was sitting there for about ten minutes when I decided to get out of the car and go see what was taking her so long to come out. I didn't want to be late for service. I left the engine running.

I knocked on the door twice and she slowly opened it. She was wearing a black scarf on her head and the same black robe that she had on when I was there before.

"Kiana, are you going to church?"

"No, I'm not going?"

"Is everything okay? You sick?"

"No."

"What's wrong?"

"I think that you and I should talk," she said.

"About what?"

She nodded for me to come inside. I took a few steps into her apartment and the screen door slammed behind me.

"I heard that you and Carla got engaged."

"Yes."

"I don't understand how you could even think about marrying

her!"

"Excuse me?"

"You heard me," she barked. "Are you playing some kind of game here?"

"What are you talking about?"

"I thought that you were just having your fun with her and that eventually you would come around," she argued. "You men do that stuff all the time."

"Carla and I were together long before you even moved to Utica."

"Doesn't matter," she said and hissed. "The only reason you like her at all is because of how she looks."

"That's not true!"

"It is true," she shouted. "Have you even prayed about it? What does God have to say about it?"

"Look, I'm not having this conversation with you!"

"Cause you know I'm right!" she hollered. "This is the stupidest thing I have ever heard!"

"Kiana, you and I are not involved. We have never been together like that. I've never given you reason to think otherwise."

"That's because you won't open your eyes to what's standing right in front of you. People miss God all the time."

"What are you even saying?" I questioned.

"You and Carla don't make sense like you and me, and you know this!" she screeched.

"Look you need to calm down," I directed.

"No, you need to listen!" she demanded. "Even Carla knows that I'm better for you. That's why she got mad at me for giving you a Bible for Christmas. She's already jealous of us."

She looked crazed – an unholy alliance of anger and desperation.

"Look, I have had enough of this nonsense," I said as I stepped back further and threw both of my hands up in the air. "You have clearly lost your mind."

I turned to leave, and she grabbed my arm.

"Please don't touch me!" I demanded as I quickly pulled my arm and shoulder from her grasp. Now I was angry too.

"Okay, okay," she replied. "Just please don't go. I just want to talk. Sam, please don't go!"

She was laser-focused like a cat in the wild about to strike. I felt like prey. My heart was beating like a drum. Everything in me was telling me to get out of there.

"Kiana, you need help," I spoke softly. "You need to see someone. I'm going to go to the church and tell Pastor Marlene that…"

"I don't care who you tell!" she roared. "I love you and we are supposed to be together!"

"You don't love me. I objected. "You don't even know me."

"Yes, I do!" she insisted. "I see you in my dreams every night. I know what God told me about us."

"C'mon Kiana. God didn't tell you anything about me. He would never give you someone who belongs to someone else."

"You don't belong to her!"

"That's my decision to make."

"Why don't you come inside and sit down, and I will make you see," she implored. "I can prove it to you."

She suddenly opened her robe and let it drop to the floor, revealing her naked body.

"Oh, my God!" I reacted. "What are you doing?"

"I'm trying to get you to wake up, Sam. I know you want me."

"I'm getting out of here!" I exclaimed. "Please stay away from me!"

I turned and hurried out the door. I never looked back. I made a mad dash the few feet to my car and sped off. I was in disbelief about what had just happened. Kiana was clearly having some kind of emotional breakdown. It occurred to me that she might be suicidal.

I drove to the church with the intention of telling Pastor Marlene what just happened. Unfortunately, both pastors were out of town. There was a guest speaker, a Black guy, who was a friend of Pastor Justin from Bible college. When I arrived, he was just beginning his message. I sat in the back of the sanctuary and tried to listen. But I didn't hear a word of the sermon as I kept replaying the scene with Kiana over in my head.

I was glad when the service finally ended. It felt like torture sitting there. After the benediction, I immediately headed for the door.

"Hey, Sam," a male voice spoke and interrupted my erratic thoughts.

His was another familiar face, whose name I couldn't recall. He was an older white guy with mostly grey hair. I knew that he always came to the men's meetings, but I couldn't remember ever speaking to him directly."

"Hi," I replied.

"What made you sit back here with us common folk?" He smiled bright and his deep blue eyes caught my attention.

"Oh, I was just late, and I was too embarrassed to walk all the way up front to where I normally sit."

"Well, it's good to have you."

"Thank you."

"Is there something wrong? he inquired. "You don't look so good."

"Yeah, I'm okay."

"You sure?"

"Something that just happened with someone caught me off guard."

"Isn't it maddening how the Holy Spirit insists on testing us right when we are busy doing something?"

"What?"

"Struggles are tests, right?" he asked. "They only come to make us strong."

"*Strong?*"

"Yeah, faith is a muscle that must be regularly stressed to grow. The Bible says that '*our faith is tested by fire.*'"

"I guess it does say that" I admitted.

"I joke with my wife all the time that I am battle tested for sure. I try to look for God during my storms to see what he is trying to teach me."

"That's probably a really good way of looking at it."

"Sam, I don' know what just happened and I'm not asking you about it cause I don't need to know. But just make sure you see it for what it is. As God's people who are called by his name, he works through us to accomplish his will on the earth and to reach those who are hurting and lost. That means we trust that he will work out everything for our good and that we are not afraid, even if it costs us everything we hold dear- even our lives."

"I just don't know how to do that," I conceded. "It's harder than it looks."

"Ain't that the truth?" he said with a little grin. "Son, just try not to let someone else's' weaknesses cause you to stumble and fall. How we respond to our challenges is everything because unbelievers are watching us, and we are the only *Jesus* that many of them will ever see. And God is always good."

"I know that God is good," I replied. "I just have a hard time with the part about him being *good all the time.*"

"It's a matter of perspective and from where we stand, we can't possibly see or know it all," he contended. "Now, can we?"

I didn't respond. The question seemed rhetorical, and I was running out of words.

"Mind if I pray for you, brother?" he asked.

"No, I don't mind."

He put his hand on my shoulder and prayed:

"Heavenly, Father. Thank you for your Holy Spirit that leads and guides us in all truth. We ask that you give Sam wisdom and insight into this thing that is troubling his spirit. Let him know your heart in the matter and help him to be obedient to do the things that are pleasing to you. We trust that his very steps are ordered by you. I also feel impressed right now Father to also pray that you will send your angels now to protect Sam's physical health. I thank you that your word is true and that no weapon formed against us shall prosper. These and all blessings, we ask and pray in the name of Jesus."

"Thank you," I whispered, and we briefly man-hugged. "I really appreciate it."

"You know, Sam, the world is full of beautiful colors. Everywhere you look there are things rich and vibrant in color...truly spectacular! That's because God loves variety."

"I'm sure he does," I agreed.

"But it's impossible to see color fully when we are standing in the dark."

"I don't understand."

"Just keep on living," he charged. "You'll see."

Suffice it to say, I left the church in a much better frame of mind than I had when I first arrived. I was grateful that I belonged to a church where people truly cared about each other. I couldn't help but wonder how much further I would have progressed in my life and faith walk if I had this kind of support when I was growing up in the inner city.

I knew that I needed to tell Carla about Kiana as soon as possible. I didn't want Kiana making a scene at the news station in front of everyone. The problem was that it was hard to get ahold of Carla on the weekends. All I could do was leave her a message to call me.

I also knew that this would be very upsetting for her at a time that should have been one of the happiest seasons in our lives. She was still soaring high the last time I saw her. We both were. The impromptu family celebration at her parent's house was fun, and everyone was so happy for us. We were floating on cloud nine.

Her mother promptly informed us that we couldn't get married for at least a year because *she* needed that much time to plan a "proper" wedding. She also insisted that we get married in Rochester and that it had to be a "decent" size wedding because she considered small weddings to be in poor taste. We both just sat quietly together and listened politely to her demands while secretly mocking her behind her back like two eighth graders.

I watched Carla on the news. She was so good and looked beautiful. I could hardly believe my good fortune in finding this incredible woman. I tried to call her as soon as she was off the air, but just as I figured, I had to leave a message with some woman for her to call me.

However, she never called me before I went to bed at midnight. Honestly, I was a little relieved because I didn't know how to tell her what happened, especially over the phone. But my spirit was stirred, and I ended up tossing and turning in bed most of the night.

Chapter 29

I have always been an early riser. Even as a teen, I never needed an alarm clock to get me up in the morning. Usually, I awakened around 7:00 am every morning, prayed quickly, and jumped out of bed to start my day. But this day was different, I felt sick to my stomach as soon as I opened my eyes. The last thing I wanted to do was move my body anywhere. It was so odd because I felt fine the night before.

I somehow managed to drag myself out of bed and headed to the bathroom. I was completely out of sorts. I hoped that a hot shower would help me find my bearings, but I felt worse standing there, so I quickly got out of the shower, dried off and threw myself on the bed faced down. I went back and forth in my head considering whether I should go to work before my screaming headache made the final decision for me.

When I reached for my phone, my intention was to call the office. Instead, I dialed Carla's number. She didn't answer. I felt a weird sense of urgency to talk to her, so I hung up the phone and I immediately called her again. There was still no answer.

I forced myself to get up again and to get dressed. I tolerated a couple of sips of coffee, and I felt a little better. The cool morning air on my face seemed to help too. Although I wasn't reckless, I drove as fast as I could to Carla's place.

There were a lot of cars parked on both sides of the two-way street, and Carla's car was parked on the street in front of her apartment. I drove past it, and I found a parking spot on the next block. I got out of my car and moved at a pretty good clip to her front door. I knocked several times.

"Carla!" I called out.

She didn't answer. I didn't hear anything inside. I tried to turn the knob, but the door was locked. I was feeling anxious, and I knocked hard a few more times.

"Carla, please open the door!"

Still nothing.

"Carla!" I shouted.

I turned and started walking fast back to my car. That's when I saw the small white Volkswagen Beetle parked directly across the street from me facing the opposite direction. It looked out of place because it wasn't properly aligned with the other cars. I remembered that Mama said that Kiana had a little white car with a big dent in front. I could clearly see the front-end damage on the car. My heart almost leaped out of my chest, and I bolted back to Carla's apartment.

"Kiana, I know you're in there!" I shouted. "Open this door now!"

There still was no response.

"Kiana, I'm calling the police if you don't open the door this second! I mean it!"

The only thing I could hear was the sound of my own heart beating.

"Kiana!"

For a few incredibly long seconds there was nothing. And then the door opened slowly. It was now slightly ajar. Instinctively, without hesitation, I pushed it all the way open and stepped inside.

I didn't see anyone at first as my eyes adjusted to the different lighting. I took a few steps forward and I heard a quiet whimper. I turned and I saw Carla sitting on the floor in the middle of the living room. She looked terrified. She was wearing a purple t-shirt and pajama bottoms. Her left eye was red and swollen and her bottom lip was busted. There also was a small amount of blood present in the corner of her mouth. I started to go to her when I heard the door slam behind me.

I turned to see Kiana standing there. In her right hand was what appeared to be a gravity knife with a 6-inch blade. She was wearing a white hooded sweatshirt and jeans. Her braids were wild on her head, and she looked like a menacing caricature of herself.

"Kiana, what's going on?"

"What are you doing here, Sam?"

"What the hell are you doing?" I shouted.

"What does it look like?" she asked with a smirk.

"C'mon Kiana, I don't think you want to do this!"

"Don't you dare tell me what I want!" she ordered.

I started to move toward her, and she lifted the knife and pointed it directly at me.

"Don't be stupid, Sam," she warned. "I'm from Brooklyn. I will slice and dice you into a hundred pieces before you know what hit you."

"Kiana what did we do to you?" Carla pleaded.

"Shut up!" Kiana erupted and her whole body shook with emotion. "The next time you speak to me, girlie, will be your last time saying anything in this life. You hear me?"

Carla froze in place. I gestured to her with my hand to settle.

"Kiana, can't we just talk about this?" I implored.

"I begged you to talk to me yesterday, and you ran away like a scared little girl. Now you want to talk to me, Sam?"

"Yes, I do."

"Get on the floor!" she demanded.

"What?"

"I said get down on the floor next to her. You love her so much, then maybe I'll send y'all both to hell together!"

I hesitated.

She started to move towards me, and I raised both of my hands in surrender and dropped down onto the wooden floor. I slowly scooted over in front of Carla facing Kiana.

"That's a good boy… So now, what do you want to talk about, Sam?" she taunted. "I'm curious. What do you got to say?"

"I don't understand why you are so angry with me," I appealed.

"I threw myself at you and all you could think about was that little Black barbie doll over there. You had your chance to get it right and you blew it!"

"Please don't say that" I begged. "I know now that I made a mistake."

"Huh…You don't mean it," she challenged.

"I thought about what you said all night," I contended. "I was blinded by other things. You were right. I wasn't listening to my spirit."

"I don't believe you," she pushed back. "You are just trying to trick me. I saw the look on your face yesterday. You think I'm crazy. I'm not that stupid."

"I don't think you are stupid at all."

"Yes, you do!" she roared. "I should probably cut her cold heart out first and feed it to you. What do you think about that?"

"Kiana, yesterday you said you loved me," I shifted. "Did you mean it or was it all just a big lie?"

"... Not anymore... I did love you."

"But what if I love you too."

"What?"

"I said I love you too."

"You don't love me."

"I was just scared," I explained.

"Scared of what?"

"People not understanding how I could be so torn between the two of you."

"That's what I was trying to say too," she vented. "She could never love you like I do!"

"I didn't know how you felt," I said. "You never said anything."

"Marlene said I couldn't tell you. But I really wanted you to know."

"And now that I do know, it changes everything," I said.

"…No, it's too late. I was forced to…"

"Either you love me, or you don't," I interjected.

"You're all I ever wanted," she replied.

"If you love me, then you need to trust me."

"I want to trust you," she cried.

"There can be no real love without trust?" I presented.

"… I don't know how…"

"You can't be afraid to take chances. Not if you want the real thing."

"I'm not afraid," she claimed.

"We trust God and we trust people. Remember we talked about this that day in my car?"

"Yes, I remember."

"Then put the knife down so that we can settle this for once and for all. This is all my fault, not yours or Carla's. Let me try to make it right."

She just stood there in place, dazed.

"Please, Kiana, can't we start over?"

"I don't know," she said and looked down at the shiny knife as if she just remembered she had it.

"Yes, you do," I urged. "Please, I know I hurt you. I'm so sorry."

I slowly stood to my feet, took one step forward and opened my arms wide. I could see her thinking as the tension in the room rose to a fever pitch. She only hesitated for a moment before walking into me. We held each other tight. I felt her strong heartbeat as she pressed her body close to mine. She gently kissed my neck, and I felt the heat of her warm breath tickle as she exhaled and cried softly.

"I'm sorry too, Sam," she whispered in my ear.

I felt something else... lower. It mostly felt like a little pressure or popping on my left side. It was just enough to cause me to lose my balance, and I fell forward on top of her as we both toppled to the floor. Seizing the moment, I grabbed a handful of the braids on the left side of her head with my right hand and I slammed her head twice into the floor as hard as I could. She groaned as she lost consciousness.

As I rose to my feet, my only thought was of Carla. I turned to face her. The last thing I remember is hearing her piercing scream, which echoed in my head like an atomic bomb exploding.

Chapter 30

I woke up in recovery. Everything was white. I thought I was dead. When I attempted to rise, a woman came to my bedside and pushed me back down. She was telling me to stay calm and to lie still. Someone else appeared.

"Sam."

"Carla?"

"Yes, it's me... oh, Sam!"

"What's going on?" I asked. "They won't tell me."

"You're in the hospital?"

"Me? No, I'm not. What happened?"

"You got stabbed."

"Stabbed?"

"Yes, but you're okay now," she spoke through bated breath and a sea of tears.

"What happened to your eye?" I questioned. "Did you get stabbed too?"

"No, it's nothing," she answered. "How do you feel?"

"I'm okay? Are you okay, Carla?'

"Yes, Sam. I'm okay."

"Good, cause I want you to be okay."

"I want you to be okay too," she whispered.

"I told you that I'm okay so you can stop crying now."

———•●•———

I opened my eyes, and someone was fidgeting with some tubes that were over my head. It took me a few seconds to remember where I was.

"Sam?" the nurse called out in a strong voice. "You awake? You awake?"

I was trying to focus my eyes.

"Hi Sam," Carla suddenly appeared again.

"Hi," I answered.

"How do you feel?"

"Um, I don't know."

"Does anything hurt?" the nurse asked.

"My leg hurts."

"How bad?" she pressed.

"Bad," I replied.

"Okay, your doctor is here doing rounds. I'm going to tell him that you're awake."

"Okay."

"Sam."

"Mama?"

"How you doing, son?"

"I'm okay Mama. How did you get here?"

"Carla came and got me."

"Oh."

"I don't know if I ever been so scared about anything in my whole life," she said.

"I'm sorry, Mama."

"It's not your fault," she replied. "I told you that girl was up to something."

"We are not going to talk about that now," Carla deflected. "The important thing is that Sam is going to be alright."

"You right," Mama agreed. "I know I talk too much."

Just then the doctor walked in. He was a middle-aged white man in a white coat.

"Hello. Sam. They tell me that you just woke up from your little nap. My name is Dr. Miller. Do you remember what happened to you?"

"No, not really."

"You were stabbed in your groin area here," he explained and pointed. "There was only one puncture wound about 4 inches deep. It nicked your femoral artery, and that's why there was so much bleeding. We had to go in to repair it. The surgery went well, and you should make a full recovery."

"Did you do the surgery?" I asked.

"No, Dr. Katz did, but I was there for some of it."

"How long is the recovery period?" "Hard to say… maybe 3 to 4 months."

I did a double take. "How long?"

"It's a serious injury. You could have died."

"How long will I have to be in the hospital?"

"About a week I'd say. We just want to make sure that no infection sets in anywhere."

"Okay?"

"Any more questions? Anyone?"

"Um…That's my grandson," Mama spoke up. "Will he still be able to have kids?"

"Yes," Dr. Miller said. "I don't think that will be a problem."

"I was just asking cause they're getting married."

"Congratulations," the doctor said. "All things considered; I'd say you're a pretty lucky man. This injury could have been a lot worse. I ordered something for the pain. Let us know if you need anything else."

"Thank you," I said.

"You're welcome," he replied and turned and walked out.

"Sam, why don't you try to get some rest?" Carla asserted.

"What time is it?" I wondered.

"It's a little after midnight."

"How long have you been here?"

"I don't know."

"Maybe you should go home."

"That's what I've been trying to tell her," Mama reported. "I can stay here with you. I promise you I ain't going nowhere. Ain't no sense in both of us sitting here."

"I think you should both go home," I said. "I'll be fine."

"I can't go back to my apartment tonight," Carla answered. "My mom is coming tomorrow to help me clean the mess, but I don't want to go back there tonight by myself."

"Then come home with me," Mama interjected. "You're family now. I'll take good care of you."

"Well, I don't know…," Carla hesitated.

"We can come back first thing in the morning," Mama said. "You have to get your rest too. You're just gonna make yourself sick too and what good is that going to do?"

"Alright, if you're sure." Carla looked to me for reassurance.

"Good, then it's settled," Mama decided.

"Okay," Carla said.

I reached out for her hand, and she took mine.

She kissed me on the side of my face. I could see that her eyes were beginning to fill with tears.

"Go get some rest," I whispered. "I'll be here when you get back. I promise."

"I love you," she said.

I felt her words again touch my soul, even being laid up the way I was.

"I love you," I replied.

Chapter 31

I dreamed that I was a kid again and that I was in my room in bed sleeping. A familiar ominous presence was standing over me looking down. It was a reoccurring visitor from my past who regularly haunted my nights. I never told anybody.

"Sam?"

"Sam?"

I opened my eyes. The room was mostly dark. Only a small light behind me slightly illuminated half of it.

"I'm sorry to have to wake you," the nurse pleaded. "But there is a woman downstairs causing a little bit of commotion with security. She says that she is your mother, and she is demanding to come up. We will let her in if that is okay with you. She said that her name is Janet Hicks?"

"It's okay," I said.

"Visiting hours are over," she explained. "I just had to check with you first. I'm sorry."

"No problem. Thanks."

I dozed again. When I opened my eyes, Janet was standing in the shadows at the foot of the bed.

"Hi," I said.

"Hi."

"You can come closer." I directed.

She moved slow and exhaled loudly as she inched in. I couldn't see her face clearly, but I thought she looked scared. I never saw her look scared before.

"Um… how you feeling?" she whispered.

"I'm alright."

"I just heard about what happened."

"The doctor said that I will be okay."

"Good, um… I…"

"I'm glad you came," I offered.

"You are?"

"Yes, I am."

"I woulda came sooner, but I had to find a ride."

"No problem. You're here now."

"Does it hurt?"

"A little. They have me on a lot a pain medicine."

"Why did that girl do this to you?"

"She was jealous."

"Jealous of you and the pretty girl on the news?"

"Yes, we're getting married."

"You are? When?"

"Next year."

"I wish ya'll my best. I really do."

"Thank you," I said. "I want you to come to our wedding."

"Me?"

"Yes."

"Oh, I don't know about that," she said and put her head down.

"Why?"

"Cause I know I embarrass you."

"I never said that."

"You didn't have to," she resisted. "I know what you think."

"Mostly, I think I have just been mad at you for most of my life."

"What you mad for? I never did anything to you."

"Listen, I don't want to fight," I deflected.

"I don't want to fight with you either," she maintained. "I came here cause I was worried about ya."

"I know," I replied softly. "And I appreciate that. It means a lot."

"I did the best I could with you and the twins," she maintained. "I always made sure you was safe. Nobody can say I didn't."

"I just wish that you could have been there more. That's all I'm trying to say."

"I was there probably more than you think I was," she snapped.

"Right."

"I was!" she raised up. "I don't care what Mama told you. She always knew where I was."

"Mama hasn't told me anything and this has nothing to do with her," I expressed. "This is about me and you. I want us to have a better relationship, and I was wondering if there was a way that we could be friends?"

Her eyes shot open wide. "You wanna be friends with me?"

"Yes, I really do."

"But why?"

"Because you are my mother, and I don't really know you."

"I don't know you either," she shot back.

"That's what I'm saying. Can't we just start fresh and start learning who both of us are?"

"Um… are you being for real right now?" she questioned.

"Yes, I am," I declared. "A brand-new beginning for us- me

and you. What do you say?"

She hesitated. In that moment, she looked like a lost little girl.

"…Please," I begged. She was a lot like a wounded stray animal. I needed to go slow.

"I forgive you," I whispered.

She gasped loudly and froze in place.

"So, can we?" I nudged.

"…Well, I never heard anything like this before and…"

"Hi, my name is Sam," I interrupted. I put my arm over the rail and extended my hand to her. I held my hand steady.

"Ah…I'm Janet," she answered. She gave me her hand and briefly looked directly at me before quickly averting her eyes. When she attempted to pull away, I didn't let go of her hand and I held on to it for a few more seconds. She was shaking noticeably. I gave her a reassuring nod and I thought I saw her smile a little.

"So, how did you know that I was here anyway?" I wondered.

"Um…it was Mama. She must have had half of Utica looking for me."

I smiled to myself.

I was very tired from the surgery and kept dozing off throughout the night. I tried to get her to go home, but she refused to leave. She sat quietly in the stillness, which I knew was hard for her to do.

I woke up in a lot of pain. There was a burning sensation just above my left knee that seemed to get more intense by the minute. I told the nurse that the pain was getting bad, and she was supposed to be getting me something. But she seemed to be taking her sweet time doing it. I could feel my whole body tense up.

Janet pushed the button for the nurse, who eventually came back.

"Where is the pain stuff?' she abruptly asked.

"We're still working on it."

"What's that supposed to mean?"

"We need a doctor's orders, and we can't find it."

"That sounds like a personal problem to me," Janet attacked.

"We are doing our best," the nurse claimed. "Please be patient."

"Oh, I don't think so," Janet replied. "Let me tell you something. You have exactly one minute to get my son some pain medicine before all hell breaks loose up in here. Do you understand me?'

"Yes, mam."

"One minute!" she barked. "Now go! And you probably need to be runnin'."

Whatever the doctor gave me worked nicely and I immediately fell back into a sound sleep until I was awakened again by more of their prodding and poking. I never heard Carla come in the room. She brought her mother and my grandmother with her. I had no idea how long they had been there.

"How are you?" Carla whispered and kissed me.

"I'm good. How are you?"

"I'm good too," she said. "How did you sleep?"

"Good. How long have you been here?"

"We got here about twenty minutes ago. Sam, people have been calling all morning. Everyone from your job and your church and everywhere. It's been wild!"

"Hi, Sam," it was Carla's mother. "I'd say you look great all things considered."

"Thanks."

"I didn't know you were a celebrity," she said. "I should have guessed."

"Have you met Janet, my mother?" I asked.

I looked over at Janet who was sitting next to Mama. She rose up a little at the mention of her name.

"Yes, we were just having a nice talk."

"We was just talking about the wedding," Mama stated.

"Yes," Mrs. Jenkins said and smiled bright. "We have quite a few plans for you, so you need to hurry up and get your strength back. We'll have none of this laying around."

"Okay," I replied.

Chapter 32

I was in the hospital for five days, and that was about all I could take. It hurt a little to lie on my left hip and to walk, but otherwise, I felt fine. If I had my way, I would have gone back to work right away, but the women in my life decided that that was out of the question.

Kiana was in the county jail. She was in the hospital too for a couple of days with head and neck injuries. They charged her with attempted murder, along with several other serious felonies. I wasn't sure what I thought about that, but I knew that I didn't want her to be in prison for a long time. Mostly, I just wanted her to get the help that she needed.

"How come you didn't tell me that Kiana was infatuated with you?" Carla asked one night at my apartment.

"Because I wasn't sure what she was." I answered. "I mean, I wasn't interested in her at all."

"I know that, but I think that all of this could have been avoided if I would have cut her off from the beginning."

"She really wasn't too outrageous until recently. But I did tell you that I didn't want to be around her."

"Yes, but I wasn't hearing it like that," she defended. "It scares me to find out that she's been hating me behind my back all this time."

"I'm not sure that she hates you," I opined. "She let her sickness eat away at her like a parasite She should have gotten treatment for her mental health."

"I feel like I can't trust anybody."

"You can trust me," I maintained.

"I didn't mean you."

"How did she react when you told her that we were engaged?"

"I thought she was happy. She jumped up and down and gave me a big hug and talked about going shopping with us for my dress."

"That's amazing," I contended.

"Why?"

"Because the engagement is the thing that sent her off the deep end," I reflected.

"Can I ask you something?" she shifted.

"Go ahead."

"How did you know that I was in trouble?"

"Ah, I don't really know," I pondered. "I just kind of sensed that something was wrong."

"*Sensed*?"

"Uh huh."

"With me?'

"I thought I heard you crying," I disclosed. "It made me sick to my stomach."

"*Sick*?"

"Uh huh."

She sat perfectly still momentarily.

"I thought that you were going to think that I was insane or something when I showed up at your door in a panic first thing in the morning."

"I had no idea how far I'd let you in," she articulated. "It's hard for me to wrap my mind around how safe I feel with you."

"I told you I got you girl."

"Yeah, you did tell me that," she said under her breath.

She cupped her chin in her right hand as she leaned slightly to the right in the chair.

"What else?" I asked. "What are you thinking about?"

"About how you literally risked your life for me."

"Ah, you're making it bigger than what it was," I cautioned.

"No, I'm not!"

"I'd do it a thousand times if I had to."

"Something is wrong with you," she remarked soberly. "Kiana was right, I don't deserve you."

"No, she wasn't," I refuted. "I'm the lucky one."

We stared lovingly at each other for a few moments.

"But, truthfully, none of us deserve the love of God or his many blessings in our lives," I presented. "He has favor on whom he favors."

"Seems arbitrary," she noted.

"But it's not," I opposed. "God is never arbitrary. It's not in his nature."

"You really don't think that it's a little unfair?" she questioned. "There's no rhyme or reason why some women have multiple relationships and marriages, and others can't even find one good man to date, let alone to love. I know I feel bad."

"We can't feel guilty because we have something that other people don't," I argued.

"I feel bad because all Kiana wanted was for someone to love her," Carla clarified. "That's not a bad thing."

"Unfortunately, a lot of women feel that way," I said. "I know it hurts. But sometimes it hurts just being Black, or whatever your thing happens to be. We all have crosses to bear. But women bleed differently for sure."

"Aww…look at my man being all sensitive," she replied and touched my face.

"I'm learning."

"Yes, I can see," she affirmed.

"None of the women in the house I grew up in ever really had a *good man* to call their own. Every guy they got involved with was more trifling than the last, including my own father. I've seen it my whole life, up close and personal. It was painful to watch."

—•●•—

Pastor Justin called me the first night that I was released from the hospital, and we talked for a long time. He said that they had tried to see me in the hospital the first night but were turned away by the police.

"Sam, I can't tell you how bad we feel about this entire ordeal. We feel responsible somehow."

"*Responsible*? Why?"

"Because we were probably over our heads with Kiana," he admitted. "We probably should have insisted that she get professional help."

"In hindsight maybe, but you had no way of knowing what was going on her head."

"No, we didn't."

"She put up a pretty good front," I said.

"Yes, I guess she did. Marlene is really kicking herself."

"Can you maybe do me a favor?" I asked.

"Yes, anything."

"Could you go to the jail and check in her?" I inquired. "My guess is that she hasn't had anyone visit her."

"You want me to visit the woman who tried to *kill* you?" he replied in disbelief.

"Yes, she's a member of your church, isn't she?" I presented.

"Yes."

"And God still loves her, right?" I pressed.

"Yes, he most certainly does."

"And he hasn't given up on her?"

"No, I don't believe that he has."

"There is a deep well of pain there," I related. "I saw it clearly, boiling and churning over. It was hellish… She doesn't have any family here and I think that she could probably use a friend right about now. Don't you?"

"I think that's incredibly generous of you," he reflected. "We will get right on that."

"Thank you," I said.

"Sam is there anything that I can do for you?" he asked.

"Me?"

"Yeah."

"I can't really think of anything," I contended. "I'm good."

"Are you sure?" he asked in earnest. "You have really been through a lot. You must have… questions. You didn't deserve any of this."

"I know that" I agreed. "But lately I've been thinking a lot about everything that I have been through, not just recently, but, you know, in my whole life, and you know something, Pastor?"

"What's that?"

"I *believe* God," I said.

"What?"

"Now that I know him better, I *believe* him."

"It's written in the Bible that '*Abraham believed God and it was counted to him as righteousness,* '" Pastor Justin quoted.

"Right, but all I really know is I can't think of one person in the whole world who I would say is more loved by God than me-not one," I declared. "Amazingly, I have finally learned to trust him with everything, even my life."

"I couldn't be happier for you," Pastor encouraged. "I can clearly see that God has *shined* his face on you!"

"I know he has," I acknowledged. "And it's a whole new world."

————•●•————

Between Carla and Mama, I thought I was going to lose my mind. They called me several times a day, treated me like a child and wouldn't let me do anything for myself. While I really did appreciate their concern, I wasn't used to having to answer to anyone. My friend Larry said for me to consider it practice for when Carla and I were married.

"She owns you, brother," he teased. "So, just take it like a man!"

Carla wouldn't let me drive, so she was spending more time at my apartment. I didn't mind having her there, but I was starting to get a little worried about her.

"Are you still afraid to be alone in your apartment?" I asked during a midweek dinner at my place.

"Not particularly, why do you ask?"

"Because everyone seems to be focusing on me, but you went through the same trauma, maybe even worse. I don't really remember that much of what happened after I got to your apartment."

"You were so brave!" she remarked.

"So, how are you really?" I intreated.

"At first, I felt guilty and stupid for not seeing what Kiana was doing, but I talked about all of it with my therapist and she walked me through most of it."

"Really?"

"She thinks that Kiana probably suffers from borderline personality disorder, which explains her crazy mood swings and her tendency to mask her true feelings and emotions. I think that she was different with me than she was with you."

"I would agree with that."

"Looking back, I can see that she has an intense fear of abandonment or ending up alone," she concluded.

"She attacked you physically," I shifted. "I hate the thought of that."

"Yeah, but I think the worst part for me was seeing her stab you," she recounted, and her eyes filled with tears. "If I close my eyes, I can still see it all happening in slow motion … and all of the blood."

"I'm sorry that you had to witness that."

"Thank you, but I don't want you to worry about me," she demanded. "I'm not fragile and you know I hate it when people treat me like I'm made of glass. Maybe for the first time in a long time, I'm in a much better place."

"I'm happy for you…and me," I replied.

"Me too." She jumped to her feet and went into the kitchen to get coffee.

"But my mother is trying to push me over the edge," she stated upon her return. "The woman is obsessed with the wedding I tell you!"

"Maybe we should just run away and get married," I proposed. "Forget about all this other stuff."

"She would never speak to either one of us again," Carla

prophesied straight-faced using a monotone. "And I'm being completely serious right now."

"Well, it's our wedding, not hers," I foolishly expressed.

"Now you're talking like a crazy person," she asserted. "Our job is to show up on the appointed date and time and stand where she tells us to stand and smile like living statues. Got it?"

She poked me on the arm.

"So, it's like that?"

"You can do it the easy way or the hard way," she explained. "The choice is yours."

"Okay, if you say so."

"Other than that, we can do whatever we want."

"*Other than that?*" I reacted.

"That's the way the game is played in this here family."

"Okay, then I do have something," I said.

"What?'

"Um…" I hesitated awkwardly.

"What is it, Sam?"

I took a deep breath.

"I was thinking that… what do you think about…?"

"Just say it already!" she encouraged.

"What if we stopped… being intimate until after the wedding?"

"What? Are you serious?"

She looked bewildered.

"Yes, I am."

"But why?"

"Because I think that this is something that God is asking me to do. And I want our marriage to be *holy unto the Lord.*"

"Really?"

"Yes."

"But where did this come from?"

"Just something I've been wrestling with for a while," I confided.

"You never said anything before."

"I know," I admitted. "I thought you'd think I was losing my mind."

"So, you think that we've been doing something wrong?" she pressed.

"Uh, not really," I replied. "It's just that I didn't know anything about the ways of God when we first got together. Now I'm changing in so many ways almost every day… and seeing a lot of things differently. I know that you've seen the changes in me."

"Yes, I have."

"I think that I'll probably continue to change too, I don't know," I freely spoke. "I still have a long way to go. I just need you to understand that it doesn't have anything to do with you. I mean, I'm not rejecting you or anything about you."

"Okay."

"Loving you is easy for me, and I really believe that I was created to love you."

"Aww," she reacted and kissed me.

I reached out and held her close in my arms and momentarily lost myself.

"But no more *'tiger'?'*" she whined and gave me a little pout.

"Just until we're married and then *tiger* is coming back with a vengeance baby! You can believe that!"

"…But wait a minute," she paused. "We're talking about getting married next year at the earliest. You can wait a whole year?"

"Can *you* wait a year?" I countered. "That's the question."

"I can do it if you can," she challenged.

"Me too."

"Oh, I don't believe you," she resisted. "I think you are kidding yourself."

"Ye of little faith," I teased. "So, we got a deal?"

"Alright, it's a deal," she said slowly. "But I don't really understand why we are doing this."

"Don't worry, I'm still going to be kissing your face off, I like that. Made me laugh" I maintained.

"As long as you keep your hands to yourself, Mister," she said and waved her finger at me.

———•●•———

I had to extend my tenure in the public defender's office for another month. Tom DiLauro at the law firm graciously allowed me to change my start date there. I needed more time to tie up a couple of loose ends.

The entire staff, including Teresa, was sad to see me go. My feelings were mixed, but it was important to me to leave in the right way. Obviously, I still had high regard for the cause.

They sent a visiting judge from Syracuse to cover Judge Spinoso's cases. Judge Stone was a short, older white man with white hair who was as feisty as they come. But he also had a good heart. The contrast was striking. On the motion of the district attorney's office, he dismissed the entire indictment against Hasan. I was both thrilled and relieved. I could hardly wait to tell Hasan.

"Congratulations," I said.

"Glory be to God," Hasan praised.

"I have to say, that I'm going to miss talking to you," I stated.

"Under the circumstances, it has been an honor meeting you."

"I'm going to miss talking to you too, Mr. Hicks." Hasan expressed.

"I have learned a lot from you about what it really means to serve God with a sincere heart," I felt impressed to say.

"Thanks," he replied. "I have learned some things from you too."

I hesitated briefly before saying, "I was wondering if you wouldn't mind if I continued to come to visit you from time to time?"

"Is that allowed?" he questioned.

"Yes, that's up to me."

"Is that really something that you want to do?" Hasan wondered. "Because I know that you are a very busy man."

"You know, I never had a brother," I blurted out and looked away.

I was surprised by the growing lump in my throat.

"Me either," Hasan replied. His voice was a little shaky too.

There was an awkward silence that filled the small room like a light summer breeze on a stifling hot day.

"Ah, then…maybe… we could…" I stammered.

"Maybe we could," Hasan repeated in a quivering voice.

I rose and offered him my hand from across the table. He stood too and we shook hands on it.

I was very excited to be going back to church. It had been over a month since I was last there and I had really missed it. It was like coming home to me. I felt a little rush of adrenaline as I drove into the parking lot.

I didn't want to sit up front in the area where I used to sit with Kiana, so I went to a different section, more in the middle. My sense was that everyone was looking at me and trying not to stare. The news coverage of my stabbing was extensive. Also, everyone there knew Kiana. I understood why people were curious.

I sat on the end of the aisle. Almost immediately, an usher came up to me and handed me three printed sheets of the words of the worship songs that we were going to sing. I kept one and I gave two to Carla, who was sitting next to me, and she, in turn, handed one to Mama.

When the music started, we rose to our feet, and I could hardly contain my overflowing joy. Now, this was my jam as I was created to worship! I sang out freely from my heart because from where I was standing, God is indeed good *all the time*!

•●•

There was another news article about Judge Spinoso. The headline read: *County Court Judge Vito Spinoso removed from office by the State*. It was relatively short- only six small paragraphs. The last one read:

"The Court's order today brings a quiet but appropriate end to an attack upon justice itself, in that Judge Spinoso is removed and can never return to the bench," Commission Administrator Michael Sommerville said in a statement. "The commission appreciates that its substantive findings are undisturbed, and its removal recommendation has been implemented."

Ed Thompson is a lay minister in Syracuse, New York. He is also a trial attorney in New York, having practiced law in Syracuse for more than twenty-five years. He is a former federal prosecutor and a former assistant public defender. Additionally, Ed received a master's degree in biblical studies from Alliance Theological Seminary in 2020. Previously, Ed received a BA degree from Ohio Northern University in 1982 and a JD Degree from Albany Law School in 1985. He is the author of four legal fiction titles, including Cursed Black. Presently, he resides in Baldwinsville, New York, with his wife and daughter.